Lucy Gordon cut her writing teeth on magazine journalism, interviewing many of the world's most interesting men, including Warren Beatty, Richard Chamberlain, Roger Moore, Sir Alec Guinness and Sir John Gielgud. She's also camped out with lions in Africa, and has had many other unusual experiences that have often provided the background for her books. She is married to a Venetian, whom she met while on holiday in Venice. They got engaged within two days.

Two of her books have won Romance Writers of America RITA® Awards—*Song of the Lorelei* in 1990, and *His Brother's Child* in 1998—in the Best Traditional Romance category.

You can visit her Web site at www.lucy-gordon.com.

"Nobody else belongs here with us," she urged.

Polly gave herself up to the joy of the moment, trying to believe that only this mattered and that she could make it last forever.

It was the sound of a church bell that forced them back to reality, making them draw apart, both of them shaking with desire and confusion.

"Do you hear that?" she murmured.

"It's only the clock. Ignore it."

"I can't. It's striking midnight. Time for Cinderella to go."

"Why are you laughing?" Ruggiero asked, feeling her shaking in his arms.

"I'm laughing at myself," she said with a touch of hysteria. "Oh, heavens! I should have remembered that midnight always comes. Sensible Polly isn't always so sensible after all."

He turned her face up and looked at it in the moonlight, seeing its clean, perfect lines as never before. The sight entranced him, and he would have kissed her again, but she pressed her hands against his chest

"It's time we went home," she whispered. "The ball's over."

International bestselling author

LUCY GORDON

and
Harlequin Romance®
present

Love, marriage…and a family reunited

The Rinucci brothers are back!
Some are related by blood, some not—
but Hope Rinucci thinks of all of them as her sons.

Life has dealt each brother a different hand—some are
happy, some are troubled. But all are handsome, attractive
and successful men, wherever they are in the world.

Meet Carlo, Ruggiero and Francesco
as they find love, marriage—and each other....

Carlo's story,
The Italian's Wife by Sunset:
on sale August 07

Ruggiero's story,
The Mediterranean Rebel's Bride:
on sale October 07

Francesco's story,
The Millionaire Tycoon's English Rose:
on sale December 07

LUCY GORDON

The Mediterranean Rebel's Bride

THE
RINUCCI
BROTHERS

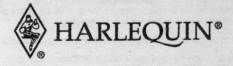

HARLEQUIN®

TORONTO • NEW YORK • LONDON
AMSTERDAM • PARIS • SYDNEY • HAMBURG
STOCKHOLM • ATHENS • TOKYO • MILAN • MADRID
PRAGUE • WARSAW • BUDAPEST • AUCKLAND

ISBN-13: 978-0-373-18326-5
ISBN-10:   0-373-18326-7

THE MEDITERRANEAN REBEL'S BRIDE

First North American Publication 2007.

CHAPTER ONE

'*I, CARLO, take you, Della, to be my wife. I promise to be true to you in good times and in bad, in sickness and in health. I will love you and honour you all the days of my life.*'

On a bright summer day in Naples, Carlo Rinucci uttered these words in the Church of All Saints and Angels. He spoke with his eyes fixed on the bride he had fought so hard to win, and behind him a quiet murmur went round the congregation.

His best man and twin brother, Ruggiero, stood quietly, waiting for the service to be over. This wedding was an unsettling experience for him.

For thirty-one years the twins had squabbled, enjoyed themselves together in various over-indulgent ways, played truant, chased girls. Though not identical, they were alike in their conviction that the race went to the swift and life was meant to be fun—and they had always acted as they were: handsome young bachelors with the world at their feet.

Now here was Carlo, dedicating himself, with quiet gravity, to a woman of frail health, seven years his senior, and doing so with the air of a man who had finally come to the place his heart desired.

Ruggiero played his part at the church perfectly, performed all his duties, then went home to the reception at the Villa Rinucci to eat and drink, flirt, and cope with the usual hearty wedding jokes,

All the Rinucci brothers were handsome, but Ruggiero had something else—the kind of outstanding looks that made him a target at weddings. A ripple would go around the female guests, combining fascination and a mysterious sense of outrage, as though no man who looked like that had any right to be on the loose.

It had been his trademark all his life: looks and charm, both with a slightly fierce edge that turned heads. He knew what was said of him, that he could have any woman he wanted, and although he enjoyed the joke he accepted it as his due.

Any woman he wanted.

Except one.

'Only you and Francesco left now,' someone said. 'I guess your mother's making plans.'

He laughed, saying, 'They won't get me.'

'You say that at every wedding,' observed his brother Luke, who was passing.

'*You* used to say it at every wedding,' Ruggiero reminded him. 'The difference is that I've held out. I'm a shining example.'

Luke paused long enough to wave to Minnie, his wife of two years, who waved back between sips of champagne.

'Just beware,' he said to Ruggiero, 'lest one day the shining example wakes up to find he's a lonely old man. Coming, *cara*.'

Ruggiero grinned, accepting this as just one of those things brothers felt obliged to say at weddings, and returned to his duties, flirting with a shy young woman until she laughed and began to enjoy herself.

When it was time for the speeches he did an excellent job, even if he said so himself—which he did. He was rewarded with looks of gratitude from Carlo and Della, and a smile of fond approval from his mother.

'You're a wonderful best man,' she said afterwards.

'Against all your expectations?' he teased.

'The only thing that surprises me,' Hope informed him, 'is that you don't have some over-painted young hussy clinging to your arm.'

'I didn't want any distractions when I had a job to do,' he explained blandly.

'Hmm!'

'Don't be so cynical, Mamma.'

'Don't be—? I have six sons, and you're surprised that I'm cynical?'

He grinned, and glided away to attend to the needs of a Rinucci great-aunt.

'Be fair to him,' Evie said, appearing at Hope's side.

She was the wife of Justin, Hope's eldest son. Before their marriage she'd been a natural rebel, caring only for her motor-bike. Happy marriage and the birth of twins had softened some of Evie's glittering edge, but had done nothing to dull the gleam of humour in her eyes.

'It's reasonable for Ruggiero to want to concentrate on his duties,' she said now.

'Reasonable?' Hope echoed. 'This is Ruggiero we're talking about.'

'I take your point,' Evie said with a laugh.

'When was he ever reasonable about anything? Working, playing, eating, drinking, hussies—everything over the top.'

'Surely his girlfriends aren't all hussies?'

'He doesn't let me meet most of them. That's how I know.' Hope sighed fondly. 'Evie, it's such a pity you can't split yourself in two—one for Justin and one for Ruggiero.'

'Maybe I wouldn't suit Ruggiero.'

'You're bound to. You're as crazy about motor-bikes as he is.'

'Is it true that he actually owns a firm that makes them?'

'Half-owns.'

'Maybe I should go and talk to him,' Evie said, laughing, and sauntered away.

It was later that evening when she caught up with Ruggiero. The guests had gone, and those family members who were staying at the villa had settled into small groups to enjoy a good natter. Justin was deep in conversation with his mother, and Evie found Ruggiero on the terrace, looking out over the lights of Naples gleaming against the darkness. With a sigh of relief she threw herself into a chair and kicked off her shoes.

'Weddings are exhausting,' she said.

He nodded. 'And there's another party tomorrow night. Mamma's never happier than when planning a big get-together. I'm going to spend the day peacefully testing a bike.'

'Ah, yes—tell me about your factory.'

He poured her a glass of wine, and sat on the low wall.

'I found the place on its last legs a couple of years ago. I knew Piero Fantone—the owner—slightly, and I bought in. Things have gone well. Our bread and butter is the standard bikes that "normal" people buy, but the specials are the racing bikes that only the "crazies" want. We've started winning races. Now we're bringing out a new racing bike, and I'm testing it tomorrow.'

'The fastest, hottest, most fearsome bike in the country,' Evie declaimed theatrically.

'Do you mind?' he said at once, in mock offence. 'In the *world*.'

'I'm sorry. But aren't there professional testers? Does the boss have to risk his neck—?' She broke off and struck her forehead. 'Oh, of course! Stupid of me. You *want* to risk your neck. Otherwise, where's the fun?'

'You've got it.' He grinned. 'Evie, you're the only woman I know who'd understand that. You should come and watch tomorrow.'

'I'd love to.' She sipped her wine and said mischievously, 'People have been talking about you all day.'

'I know. It's a bachelor's fate at a wedding.' He assumed a twittery voice of the kind he'd heard so often that day. '"He'll be next. Just wait and see."'

'Was that why you didn't bring a date?' she asked, chuckling.

'One reason. My mother complains about the girls I bring home, and when I don't bring one she complains even more.'

'I gather they're real eye-openers?'

He made a wry face, and she became serious to say, 'I guess you're a long way from finding what Carlo has.'

'I think there are very few men who find what Carlo has. Or what you and Justin have.'

She was silent, watching him sympathetically.

After a while he added, 'And thank you for not saying, *Don't worry, your turn will come*."

'Don't you think it will?' she asked, struck by the sudden quiet heaviness in his voice.

'Maybe. Or maybe it came and went.'

Evie was silent, astonished. She had always sensed that there was more to her brother-in-law than the rough, hard-living man he was on the surface, but this was the first time he'd offered so much as a hint of a more reflective inner self.

Cautiously, so not to scare him off, she said, 'Can you be sure that it's gone finally?'

'Quite sure. Since I know hardly anything about her. She was English, her name was Sapphire, and we had two weeks together. That's all.'

But it wasn't all, she could tell. During those weeks something had happened to him that had been like an earthquake.

'Do you want to talk about it?' she asked.

'I met her in London about two-and-a-half years ago. I was visiting friends, but they suddenly had a family crisis, so I left them to it and explored

London on my own. We met in the bar of my hotel. She was there to meet a friend who didn't show up, we got talking and—that was it.'

'What was she like?'

'Like something from another world. So insubstantial that I was almost afraid to touch her. I knew her for two weeks, and then she vanished.'

'Vanished? Where?'

'I've no idea. I never saw her again. Perhaps she was nothing but a mad hallucination?'

Evie was astonished. Who would have thought the hard-headed Ruggiero could talk in this way? She wondered if he even realised what he'd revealed. He was looking into the distance, his eyes fixed on some inner world. She held her breath, willing him to go on.

But instead he made a sound that was part-grunt, part-nervous laugh, seeming to draw himself back from the brink.

'Hey, what the hell?' he said edgily. 'These things happen. Easy come, easy go.'

'But I don't think it was easy,' Evie urged. 'I think she meant more to you than that.'

He shrugged. 'It was a holiday romance. How much do they ever mean?'

'Ruggiero—'

'Do you want to come with me tomorrow or not?'

'Yes, of course. But—'

'Fine. Be ready to leave early in the morning.'

He bid her goodnight and hurried to his room, despising himself for making a cowardly escape, but unable to help it. Much more of that conversation and he would have gone mad.

He stripped off his clothes and got under the shower, hoping to wash away the day. But nothing could banish the thoughts that had troubled him from the moment he'd arrived at the church with Carlo.

Carlo, the twin barely an hour younger than himself, who'd shared with him all the riotous pleasures of youth, now transformed into a man lit by a powerful inner joy. And the sight had thrown him off balance because it had called up a voice he'd thought he'd silenced long ago.

'Forget the rest of the world—there's only our world—what more do we need?'

Memories started to crowd in. She was as he'd first seen her, in a glittering tight red dress, low enough in front to show her exquisite bosom, high enough on the thigh to show off her endless legs. It was the attire of a woman who could attract men without trouble, who enjoyed attracting them and had no scruples about doing so as often as she pleased.

Within a few hours of their meeting he'd held her, naked, in his arms. Everything about her had been breathtaking—her body, the whisper of her voice, her laughter.

Other pictures crowded in: a day out together at the funfair, doing childish things. They'd sat together in a photo booth, arms entwined, heads leaning against each other, while the machine's lights flashed. A moment later two pictures had appeared in the dish, and they had taken one each.

'Sapphire,' he murmured.

It was the only name she had ever told him. She'd kept her last name a secret, and even that had been part of her magic.

Magic. He'd resisted the idea, considering himself a prosaic man and proud of it. But Sapphire had burned with erotic power, dazzling him and luring him into a furnace from which he'd emerged reborn.

She'd been an adventurous lover, who hadn't tamely waited for him in the bed but had come after him eagerly, appearing in the shower and sliding her arms around him as water laved them. How many times had he seen her shadow outside the frosted glass, then felt her beside him?

The last memory was one from which he still shied away. They'd made love in the afternoon and she'd left him in the evening, promising to return in the morning. He'd lain awake that night, vowing to bring things to a head the next day.

But the next day there had been no sign of her.

He'd waited and waited, but she hadn't appeared. One day had become two, then three.

He had never seen her again.

Now he stood in the shower, his eyes closed, keeping out the world. But at last he opened them and switched off the water.

Then he tensed.

She was there, just outside the shower, her shadow outlined on the glass. She was waiting for him.

He moved fast, hurling himself against the glass so hard that he nearly broke it, reaching out, trying to find her.

But his hands touched only air. There was nobody there. She had been an illusion as, perhaps, she had always been. He stood there alone, shaking with the ferocity of his memories.

He dried himself mechanically, trying to force himself to be calm. It shamed him to be out of control.

That was the mantra he'd lived by since the day she'd vanished into thin air. Control. Never let anyone suspect the turmoil of joy and misery that had destroyed and remade him.

He'd returned to Italy, apparently the same man as before. If his rambunctious hard living had been a little forced, his manner more emphatic, nobody had seemed to notice. He had kept his memories

a secret, sharing them with nobody in the world—
until tonight.

With Evie he'd come closer to confiding than
with anyone else, ever. But he wasn't a man who
easily discussed feelings, or even knew what his
own feelings were much of the time. So he'd gone
just so far before retreating into silence.

Today, at his brother's wedding, he'd sensed
that Carlo had found a secret door and gone
through it, closing it behind him.

For him the door had stood half-open, but then
it had brutally slammed shut in his face, leaving
him stranded in a desolate place.

All around him the villa was hushed for the
night. It was packed to the rafters with people—
many of whom loved each other, some of whom
loved him. In the midst of them he felt lonelier
than ever before in his life.

The flight from London had been delayed, and by
the time Polly landed at Naples she was feeling
thoroughly frazzled. The extra time had given her
more chance to think about what she was doing
and regret that she had ever agreed to do it.

There was a long queue to get through Passport
Control, and she yawned, trying to be patient. A
large mirror stretched the length of the wall, providing an unwelcome opportunity to anyone who

could bear to look at themselves after a flight. For herself, she would gladly have done without it. There was nothing in her appearance that pleased her.

It was wickedly unjust that, equipped with much the same physical attributes as her cousin Freda, she had turned out so differently. Freda had been tall, slender, willowy—a beauty who'd walked with floating grace. Polly was also tall and slender, but her movements suggested efficiency rather than elegance.

'And just as well,' she'd tartly remarked once. 'I'm a nurse. Who wants a nurse drifting beautifully into the ward when they need a bedpan? I run, and then I run somewhere else, because someone's hit the alarm button. And when I've finished I don't recline gorgeously on a satin couch. I collapse in an exhausted huddle.'

Freda, who'd been listening to this outburst with amusement, had given a lazy chuckle.

'You describe it so cleverly, darling. I think you're wonderful. I couldn't do what you do.'

That had been Freda's way—always ready with the right words, even if they'd meant nothing to her. Polly, prosaic to her fingertips, had seen that slow, luxurious smile melt strong men, luring them on with the hint of mystery.

To her there had been no mystery. Freda had

done and said whatever would soften her audience. It had brought her a multitude of admirers and a rich husband.

Polly had even watched helplessly as a boyfriend of her own had been enticed away from her, without a backward look. Nor had she blamed him. She hadn't even blamed Freda. It would have been like resenting the sun for shining.

Freda's heart-shaped face had been beautiful. Polly, with roughly the same shape, just missed beauty by the vital millionth of an inch. Freda's hair had been luxuriously blonde. Polly was also fair, and could probably have had the same rich shade if she'd worked on it. But life as a senior nurse in a busy hospital left her neither time nor cash to indulge her hair. She kept it clean and wore it long, her one concession to vanity.

Trapped in the slow-moving queue, she had plenty of time to consider the matter and come to the usual depressing conclusions.

'I look like I've been left out in the rain by someone who's forgotten. But is that so strange, after the way I've spent the last year?'

At last she was out, and searching for a taxi to take her to the cheap hotel she'd booked on-line, which was all she could afford. It was basic, but clean and comfortable, with friendly service. Judging it too late now to start her search, she dined in the tiny garden restaurant off the best spaghetti she'd ever tasted. Afterwards she showered and stretched out on the bed, gazing at the snapshot she'd taken from her purse.

It was a small picture, taken in a machine, and it showed Freda, gorgeous as always, sitting with a young man in his late twenties. He had dark hair that curled slightly, a lean face and a stubborn mouth. Freda was leaning against him, and his arm was about her in a gesture of possessiveness. His cheek rested on her head, and although he was half smiling at the camera it was clear that the rest of the world barely existed for him.

Polly studied him, trying to decide why, despite his air of joy, there was a kind of fierceness about him that defied analysis. He seemed to be uttering a silent warning that Freda belonged to him, and he would defend his ownership with his last breath.

But it hadn't worked out like that. He had lost her for ever. And soon he would know it finally.

For a long time Polly lay looking at the ceiling, musing.

What am I doing here? I don't really want to see Ruggiero Rinucci, and I'm sure he doesn't want to see me.

Maybe I should have written to him first? But I don't have his exact address. Besides, some things are better face to face. Plus, men are such cowards that if he knew why I was coming he'd probably vanish. Oh, heavens, how did I get into this?

On the edge of Naples stood La Pista Grande, a large winding track that was the scene of many motorbike races.

Here, too, the firm of Fantone & Rinucci tested their motor-bikes, with Ruggiero insisting on doing all tests personally, and taking every machine to the limit.

'If it doesn't half kill him he thinks there's something wrong with it,' one of the mechanics had remarked admiringly, and when Ruggiero was on the track as many as possible of the workforce turned out to watch, cheer and take bets on his survival.

He arrived next morning with Evie, gave her some technical paperwork about the bike and showed her to the best place in the stands, just where the track curved three times in a short space, so that briefly he would be riding straight for her before turning into another sharp bend.

'If I break my neck, it'll likely be just there,' he said, indicating the mechanics who were also there. 'That's why they gather in this spot— hoping.'

Evie laughed. There was a sprinkling of women among the mechanics, and she doubted if they'd come hoping for an accident. More likely it was connected to the sight of Ruggiero in tight black leather gear that emphasised every taut line of his tall, lean but muscular figure.

He gave a harsh grin and departed, leaving Evie to get to her seat in the front row. As she was settling she became aware of a young woman standing a few feet away. She was slim, with long fair hair and a slightly nervous manner. She gave a brief smile and sat down, looking rather as though she hoped to avoid notice.

'Are you from the factory?' Evie asked pleasantly.

'No—you?'

'No, I just came to see Ruggiero. He's my brother-in-law.'

After exchanging a few more words, the stranger smiled absently and seemed disinclined to talk further. Evie took out the paperwork and plunged happily into facts and figures about sequential electronic fuel injection, adjustable preload and eccentric chain adjuster, totally absorbed until the testing was about to begin. Then she looked at the young woman and realised that she sat like stone, motionless, her eyes fixed on the track as though something vital depended on what she saw there.

Ruggiero kept his grin in place as he walked towards the two men who were holding the bike.

He used the grin as a kind of visor behind which he could hide. Today the effort was greater than usual, because he'd had little sleep. His thoughts about Sapphire had been destructive. Once conjured up, she'd refused to depart, haunting him all night until he fell into an uneasy sleep and awoke after one hour, not at all refreshed.

The sensible course would have been to delay the test until another day, but he couldn't bring himself to admit that he didn't feel up to it. Besides, he refused to give in to fancies. Sapphire could be banished if he were only resolute.

He pulled on the black helmet that enveloped his head completely, blotting out his identity and turning him into a cross between a spider and a spaceman. A kick and the engine roared into life. Another kick and he was turning out onto the track.

He took the first circuit at a mere ninety miles an hour—a moderate speed—leaning into the turn so deeply that his knee nearly touched the ground. Then he shot ahead, going faster and faster, until the machine reached a hundred and fifty—the extreme of its ability. But he knew that beyond the official limit there was always a little extra, and he urged it on, demanding just that bit more, and then more, because if he went fast enough he might outrun the ghost that pursued him.

Yet she was there, just behind him, warning

him that flight was impossible. She was there inside his helmet, telling him that she would always be with him.

But she was also ahead of him, on the track, her long fair hair fanned into a halo by the wind—waiting for him.

Suddenly all the pictures ran together, so that he could no longer see ahead. Only half knowing what he did, he turned the front wheel, desperate to avoid the apparition that might or might not be there. The next moment he was flying through the air, to land with a brutal force that knocked the breath out of him and sent the world whirling into chaos.

CHAPTER TWO

FREDA had known little about Ruggiero except that his family lived in the Villa Rinucci, and Polly would have gone there on the morning after her arrival but for the chance of the hotel receptionist leaving open a Naples newspaper with a picture of Ruggiero just visible. Knowing no Italian, she'd asked the man to translate the piece, and found a description of Carlo's wedding, with some background about the family, including a mention of the motorbike firm. She had decided to go there first, and the receptionist had called a taxi and given the driver the name of the firm.

At the factory the language problem had cropped up again, but after a certain amount of misunderstanding she'd discovered that Signor Rinucci was at the racetrack today. She'd taken the taxi on to the track, glad of the chance to observe him unseen. The place was closed to the public, but she'd arrived just as some employees of the firm were being allowed to enter through a side door, and by mingling with them she'd managed to slip inside.

As soon as she'd reached the stands she had seen him, showing a young woman to a seat in the front row. Polly had held back, wondering what place the woman held in his life. Suddenly he'd grinned, and something cold, almost wolfish about it had made her shiver. Then he'd departed and she'd been able to move down to the front row. The young woman had smiled at her.

'Are you from the factory?'

'No,' Polly said cautiously. 'You?'

'No, I just came to see Ruggiero. He's my brother-in-law.'

'You mean,' she asked in alarm, 'he's married to your sister?'

'No, I'm married to his brother.' She chuckled. 'I can't see Ruggiero ever getting married. He enjoys a wide choice of women without tying himself down.'

Polly sighed with relief. A wife or girlfriend would have made her mission much harder. She settled down to watch as Ruggiero, in the distance, mounted the fearsome looking bike, started up, gathered speed, then took off like a rocket.

Lap after lap she watched him with fierce intensity, admiring his ease in the face of danger. The track twisted and turned like a snake, so that he'd no sooner taken a bend, leaning far over to one side, than he had to swiftly straighten up and swing deep in the other direction, then back again, and again. Every move was performed with careless grace and no sense of strain.

In one place the twisting of the track brought him directly ahead, so that for a stunning moment he was heading right for her. Then he leaned deep into a terrifyingly sharp bend and was gone, vanishing into the distance, while the black visor still seemed to hang in the air before her.

Then a strange thing happened.

For no apparent reason she felt a sense of dread begin to invade her. Her brain was on red alert, saying that something was badly wrong. She knew nothing about bikes, but much about troubled minds, and every instinct told her that this man was labouring under a burden and fast reaching his limit.

She stood up, pressing against the rail, frowning as her brain tried to understand what her instincts could sense. He was right ahead again. Coming straight for her until he swung into the bend.

But it was as though he leaned in too deep and couldn't get out. The next moment the front wheel twisted, jerking the machine into a scissor-like movement that sent him flying through the air.

All around there were shouts of horror, but Polly was galvanised into action. She was first over the barrier, racing across the track, dodging the lethally spinning wheels of the bike, lying on its side, and throwing herself down by Ruggiero.

'Don't move,' she said, unsure whether he could hear her.

'Hey—' Piero Fantone had caught up and tried to pull her away.

'I'm a nurse,' she said, struggling free. 'Get an ambulance.'

'*Ambulanza!*' Piero bawled, and turned back to her.

Ruggiero gasped and made a movement. Through the dark plastic of the visor Polly saw him open his eyes, saw the stunned look in them before they closed again.

'Did he break anything?' Piero demanded.

She ran her hands lightly over Ruggiero.

'I don't think so. But I'll know better when some of this leather is removed. We need to get him inside.'

'We keep a stretcher here. It's on its way.'

From behind the visor a voice growled words she didn't understand, but the gist of them was clear to Piero, from his urgent voice and attempts to restrain him. His reward was a stream of Neapolitan words that Polly rightly guessed to be curses.

'He's all right,' Piero said.

'It's certainly reassuring,' she agreed.

Ruggiero began to fight his way up, swinging his arms wildly so that Polly, kneeling beside him, was knocked off balance. He managed to get onto one knee before keeling over and landing on her as she raised herself. She reached out quickly, supporting him as he collapsed against her, his head thrown back. For a moment she thought his eyes opened and closed again, but it was hard to be sure.

'We should take off his helmet,' she said, laying him gently back onto the ground.

Piero gently eased the helmet off, and now she could see Ruggiero clearly for the first time. It was the face in the photograph with Freda, but older, thinner, his hair disordered and damp with sweat, making him look vulnerable—something she guessed was rare for him. His eyes remained closed, but she saw his lips move.

'What's he saying?' Piero asked.

'I can't tell.' Polly leaned forward, putting her ear close. She felt the warmth of his breath against her cheek and heard a whispered name that made her tense and look at him sharply.

'Sapphire!'

'What did he say?' Piero asked.

'I—I didn't catch it. Oh, good—there's the stretcher. Let's get him inside.'

She backed away as several men lifted him and began the journey back across the track. Polly stood watching, frozen with shock, until Evie put an arm around her.

'Are you all right?'

'Yes,' she said in a dazed voice. 'Yes, I'm fine.'

'Come on—let's follow them.'

His head was full of darkness, spinning at top speed, like an endless circle. In the centre of it was her face, smiling provocatively, as so often in their time together. But then the picture changed and he saw her as she'd been at the track, standing there, luring him on until he crashed.

But then she'd appeared beside him, taking him up in her arms, pulling open his clothes, speaking words of comfort. He'd groaned, reaching out to her, and she had vanished.

He opened his eyes to find himself lying on a leather couch, with Evie beside him.

'Steady,' she said.

'Where is she?'

'Who?'

'*Her*. She was standing there—I saw her— where is she? Ouch!'

'Don't move. You had a bad fall.'

'I'm all right,' he croaked, trying to rise. 'I've got to find her.'

'Ruggiero, who are you talking about?' she asked frantically, fearful that his wits were wandering.

'That woman—she was there—'

'Do you mean the one by the track?'

'You saw her?'

'She was in the stand with me. When you crashed she rushed over and helped you.'

He stared at her, scarcely daring to believe what he heard.

'Where is she?'

'I'll fetch her. By the way, she only speaks English.'

'English?' he whispered. His voice rose. *'Did you say she was English?'*

'Yes. Ruggiero, do you think—?'

'Get her here, for pity's sake!' he cried hoarsely.

Evie slipped out.

While he waited Ruggiero tried to stand, but fell back at once, cursing his own weakness. But inwardly he was full of wild hope. It hadn't been imagination. *She* had returned, her arms outstretched to him, as so often in hopeless dreams. Now it was real. At any moment she would walk through that door—

'Here she is,' Evie said from the doorway, standing aside to usher in a young woman.

At first he saw only a tall, slender figure with long fair hair, and his heart leapt. In a movement that afterwards caused him agonies of shame, he reached out an eager hand, said her name. Then the mist cleared and he found himself looking at a face that was gentle and pleasant, but not beautiful—and not the one his heart endlessly sought.

'Hallo,' she said. 'I'm Polly Hanson. I was watching, and I'm a nurse, so I tried to help.'

'Thank you,' he murmured, dazed.

The world was in chaos. He'd thought he'd found Sapphire. Instead, here was this prosaic female whose passing resemblance was just enough to be heartbreaking. Once more Sapphire was only a ghost.

He knew he'd spoken her name—but how loud? Had they heard him? He fell back, passing a hand over his screwed-up eyes, wishing things would become clearer.

'Thank you,' he said again, forcing his eyes to open.

Piero looked in to say, 'The ambulance is here.'

'What damned ambulance?' Ruggiero roared. 'I'm not going to hospital.'

'I think you should,' Polly said. 'You have had a bad accident.'

'I landed on my shoulder.'

'Partly. Your head also took a thump, and I'd like it properly looked at.'

'*Signorina,*' Ruggiero said through gritted teeth,

'I'm grateful for your help, but please understand that you don't give me orders.'

'Well, the ambulance is here now,' she said, riled by his tone.

'Then you can send it away.'

'Signor Rinucci, your head may be injured, and I urgently suggest—'

'You may suggest what you like,' he snapped, 'but I'm not getting into an ambulance, so spare me any more of your interference.'

'Such pleasant manners,' said a voice from the door. 'It must be my son.'

Hope swept into the room.

'Mamma,' Ruggiero said painfully, 'how did you—?'

'Evie called my cellphone,' Hope said, also in English, taking her cue from the others. 'And as I was shopping nearby I had only a little way to come.'

'You just happened to be shopping nearby?' Ruggiero growled.

'Yes, wasn't it a fortunate coincidence?' Hope said smoothly.

'If you believe in coincidences.'

'Be quiet and watch your manners,' his mother said firmly. 'You've now been rude to everyone—'

'He hasn't been rude to me,' Evie observed mildly.

'Give him time. He will.'

'Especially if she mentions an ambulance,' Ruggiero retorted.

They argued. He was obdurate. In the end his mother sighed and gave in. The ambulance was sent away.

'I'll go home and rest,' Ruggiero conceded. 'And I'll be all right for the party tonight.'

'Or you may have passed out completely by then,' Polly said, with the faintest touch of acid in her voice.

Evie hastened to explain Polly's professional qualifications, and what she had done for Ruggiero.

Hope's response was to embrace Polly fervently and declare, 'We are friends for ever. So now I ask you to do one more thing for me. You must come to our party tonight.'

Beside her, Polly sensed rather than felt Ruggiero make a gesture of protest, and she knew that he didn't want her in his home. He wanted to get rid of her as soon as he could. And she could guess why.

But Hope seemed oblivious. 'Tonight I can thank you properly, and perhaps you'll also be kind enough to—' She gave her son a baleful look.

'Don't worry, I'll keep an eye on him,' Polly said.

'You will not,' Ruggiero snapped.

'Indeed I will,' she riposted at once.

'I won't have it.'

'Try to stop me.'

'That's the spirit,' Hope said, pleased. 'And, Signor Fantone, I commend you for your good sense in having a nurse at the track. I wouldn't have expected it of you.'

Having praised and insulted him in one breath, she turned her attention back to Ruggiero. With relief, Polly realised that for the moment she could avoid explanations. Sooner or later everyone would have to know why she was really here. But not yet.

Hope took charge, arranging for Ruggiero to be helped to her waiting car, and leaving Evie to give Polly a lift to her hotel.

'It's a big family get-together,' Evie explained as they drove. 'The Rinuccis tend to be scattered, but we all returned for Carlo's wedding yesterday. And, since Hope loves giving parties, she's going to have another one tonight, before we all disperse again.'

'Was it really chance that his mother was shopping nearby?'

'Of course not.' Evie chuckled. 'She does it whenever he's testing, and she always makes sure she has her cellphone, so that she can be fetched quickly if something like this happens. Of course he guesses, although he won't admit it, and it makes him grumpy. I'm sorry he was so rude to you. He isn't normally like that.'

'He was feeling bad,' Polly said, unwilling to reveal that there could be another reason for Ruggiero's hostility to her.

A few minutes later Evie dropped Polly at her hotel, promised that someone would fetch her at seven o'clock that evening, and drove off.

In her room, Polly discovered a problem. She had travelled light, wearing jeans and a sweater, and carrying enough basic clothes for a few days, but nothing that would be suitable for a party.

And I'm not turning up looking like a poor relation, she thought. I think I'll prescribe myself some shopping!

Even in that less privileged area, the clothes shops had a cheering air of fashion. A happy hour exploring resulted in a chiffon dress of dappled mauve, blue and silver, with a neck that was low enough to be 'party' and high enough to be fairly modest. The price was absurdly low. Even more absurd were the silver sandals she bought in the market just outside the hotel.

Glamorous cousin Freda, once married to a multimillionaire, would have turned her nose up at such a modest outfit, but Polly was in heaven.

As she dressed that evening she considered her

hair, and decided that it would be more tactful to pin it back.

Perhaps I should have done that this afternoon, but I never thought. He might have forgotten her—no, men never forgot Freda.

For a moment she was back by the track, watching him approach, his face unknowable behind the black visor. What had he seen? What had it done to him to bring him so close to death?

It had felt strange to hold him in her arms, the powerful, athletic body slumping helplessly against her. Vulnerability was the last thing she had expected from Freda's description.

'He had enough cocky arrogance to take on the world,' her cousin had said. 'It made me think, *That's for me.*'

'But not for long,' Polly had reminded her quietly. 'Two weeks, and then you dumped him.'

Freda had given an expressive shrug. 'Well, he'd have dumped me pretty soon, I dare say. I knew straight off that he was the love-'em-and-leave-'em kind. That was useful, because it meant he wouldn't give me any trouble afterwards.'

'Plus the fact that you hadn't given him your real name.'

'Sure. I thought Sapphire was rather good—don't you?'

What Polly had thought of her cousin's actions

was something she'd kept to herself—especially then, when Freda had been so frail, her once luxurious hair had fallen out and the future had been so cruelly plain.

That conversation came back to her now, reminding her of Ruggiero as she'd seen him first, and then later. Cocky arrogance, she thought. But not always.

He'd said Sapphire's name and reached blindly out to her before he'd controlled himself and pulled back. For him, Sapphire still lived—and that was the one thing Polly had not expected.

A chauffeur-driven car arrived exactly at seven o'clock and swept her out of the city and up the winding road to where the Villa Rinucci sat atop the hill. From a distance she could see the lights blazing, and hear the sounds of a party floating down in the clear air.

Hope came out to greet her eagerly.

'I feel better now you're here,' she said. 'Our family doctor is also a guest, but he'll have to leave soon.'

'I'd better talk to him first,' Polly suggested, and was rewarded with Hope's brilliant smile.

Dr Rossetti was an elderly man who'd been a friend of the family for a long time. He greeted Polly warmly, questioned her about her impressions that afternoon, and nodded.

'He's always been an awkward so-and-so. Now, Carlo—his twin—if *he* didn't want to do what he was told, he'd get out of it with charm, and it would be ages before you saw how he'd outwitted you. But Ruggiero would just look you in the eye and say, "Shan't!"'

Polly chuckled. 'You mean he doesn't bother with any of that subtlety nonsense?'

'Ruggiero wouldn't recognise subtlety if he met it in the street. His head has a granite exterior which you have to thump hard to make him believe what he doesn't want to believe.'

'And under the exterior?'

'I suspect there's something more interesting. But he keeps it a secret even from his nearest and dearest. In fact, especially from his nearest and dearest. He hates what he calls "prying eyes", so don't make it too clear that you're concerned for him.'

'No, I think I gathered that before,' she said wryly. She glimpsed Ruggiero across the room and added, 'From the way he's moving his left arm I think his shoulder's hurting.'

'Yes—you might find it useful to rub some of this into it,' he said, handing her a tube of a preparation designed to cool inflammation.

'And I'm sure he has concussion.'

'I doubt it's serious, since he seems well able to remember what happened. But he needs an early night. See if you can get him to take a couple of these.' He handed her some tablets.

'They might do his headache some good,' she said, nodding as she recognised them.

'Headache?' the doctor demanded satirically. 'What headache? You don't think he admits to having a headache, do you?'

'Leave him to me,' she said. 'I'm used to dealing with difficult patients.'

They nodded in mutual understanding. Then something made Polly look up to find Ruggiero watching her, his lips twisted in a smile so wry that it was almost a sneer. Of course he knew they were discussing him, and he wasn't going to make it easy for her.

Then Evie was by her side, taking her to meet the family. Carlo and Della, the newlyweds, had left for their honeymoon, but everyone else was there. While Polly was sorting out the clan in her mind, Hope appeared beside her.

'Let me take you to Ruggiero.'

'Better not,' Polly said. 'If he's expecting me to descend on him like a nanny, that's exactly what I'm not going to do.'

Hope nodded. 'You're a wise woman. Oh, dear! Why do men never listen to wise women?'

'I suppose the other kind are more fun,' Polly said with amusement. 'Let him wait and wonder.

I think I should meet some more people, just to show I'm not watching him.'

Hope took her around the room to meet the older, more distant members of the extended Rinucci clan. They all greeted her warmly, and seemed to know that she was there to look after one of their number. They were kind people, and open in their appreciation.

It didn't take long for Polly to understand that they were taking their cue from Hope, who was the centre of the whole family, a charming tyrant, exercising her will so lovingly that it was easy to underestimate her power. Toni's fond eyes followed her everywhere.

After a while Polly became aware of a glass being pressed into her hand. Looking up, she saw Ruggiero, surveying her grimly.

'It's only mineral water,' he said. 'Since I take it you're not allowed to drink on duty?'

'On duty?'

'Don't play dumb with me. You're here to fix your beady eyes on me in case I go into convulsions. Sorry to disoblige, but I'm having a great time.'

'A man with cracked ribs is never having a great time.'

'Who says I have cracked ribs?'

'You do—every time you touch your left side

gingerly. I've seen that gesture before. Often enough to know what it means.'

'And you think you're going to whisk me away to a hospital—?'

'There's no need. If you'll only—'

'Once and for all,' he said, with a touch of savagery, 'there is nothing wrong with me.'

'For pity's sake, what are you trying to prove?'

'That I'm fine—'

'Which you're not—'

'And that I don't need a nanny,' he growled.

'A nanny is just what you *do* need,' she said, coming close to losing her temper. 'In fact I never saw a man who needed it more. No—scrap nanny. Let's say a twenty-four-hour guard, preferably armed with manacles. Even then you'd manage to do something brainless.'

'Then I'm beyond help, and you should abandon me to my fate.'

'Don't tempt me,' she said through gritted teeth.

She waited for a sharp answer, but it didn't come. Looking at him, she saw why. He sat down, slowly and heavily, leaning his head back against the wall. She just stopped the glass falling from his fingers.

'Time to stop pretending,' she said gently.

For a moment Ruggiero didn't answer. He looked as if all the stuffing had been knocked out of him. At last he turned his head slowly, to look at her out of blurred, pain-filled eyes.

'What did you say?'

'I said it's time to go to bed.'

Hope appeared, looking anxious. 'What's happened?'

'Ruggiero has told me he wants to go to bed,' Polly informed her.

'Did I?' he asked.

'Yes,' she said firmly. 'You did.'

He didn't argue, but gave the shrug of a man yielding to superior forces and rose slowly to his feet. Then he swayed, and was forced to rest an arm quickly on Polly's shoulder. She heard him mutter something that she didn't understand, but she guessed it was impolite. Hope gave a signal, and at once Ruggiero's brothers appeared, taking charge of him.

'I'll come and see you when you're in bed,' Polly told him.

He groaned. 'Look, I don't think—'

'I didn't ask what you thought,' she told him quietly. 'I said that's what I'm going to do. Please don't argue with me. It's a waste of time.'

The young men wore broad grins, and the braver among them cheered. Then they caught their mother's eye, and hastily escorted their injured brother to bed.

CHAPTER THREE

POLLY gave them fifteen minutes before entering Ruggiero's room, where he lay in bed, now dressed in dark brown silk pyjamas. Hope sat beside him.

'That headache's pretty terrible, isn't it?' Polly asked sympathetically.

'You could say that,' he said in a painful whisper.

'This will make it better and give you some sleep.' She opened one hand, showing him a couple of pills, and held up a glass of water in the other.

This time he didn't argue, but struggled up and swallowed the pills, and lay back at once, eyes closed.

'He'll be better in the morning,' Polly assured Hope. 'Why don't you go back to your guests?'

'I don't like to leave him alone.'

'Don't worry—he won't be alone,' Polly said. 'I'm staying here.'

'Are you sure that—?'

Hope checked herself suddenly, and a strange look came over her face. Her children could have told her that it meant Mamma was hatching a plot, but Polly, seeing it for the first time, was merely puzzled.

'Of course you're right,' Hope said. 'I know he's safe with you.'

She gave Polly a peck on the cheek and hurried out. Polly turned out all the lights except one small lamp, and went to the window. From there she could see light as the guests spilled out into the garden. Luckily the double glazing deadened the sound, although she doubted if he would have heard anything for a while even without that.

He stirred, groaning softly, and she returned to the bed.

'It's all right,' she said. 'I'm here. Let it go.'

She could hardly have said what she meant by those words, but he seemed to understand them at once and became quiet. She drew up a chair and sat close to the bed, leaning forward to whisper, 'Let it go. There'll be time later. But for now—let her go.'

He gave no sign of hearing, so she couldn't tell if he'd heard the subtle change she'd made in the words.

One by one Ruggiero's family looked in. Some-times they spoke to her in whispers; sometimes they merely smiled. Hope opened the door quietly and stood watching Polly by the bed, her eyes fixed on Ruggiero. She waited a long time for Polly to move, then smiled, nodded to herself, and backed out, unseen.

A few minutes later Evie wheeled in a small trolley, laden with party food, plus wine, mineral water, and a pot of tea. Polly drank the tea thankfully. Tonight looked like being a two-pot problem.

Ruggiero lay without moving and she sat beside him, relieved that he seemed calm at last. When she was sure he was resting properly she rose and crossed again to the window. It was now quiet enough for her to risk opening it and looking out to where the last of the guests were drifting into the cars that would take them away, waving goodbye to Hope and her husband Toni.

She was about to draw back when another car drew up. The driver got out and pulled a bag from the back seat, showing it to Hope, who made a gesture of satisfaction.

Then Polly stiffened and leaned out further, frowning as she recognised the bag as her own, and the truth dawned on her. Hope had sent someone to the hotel to bring her things here—and she'd done it without so much as a by-your-leave.

Toni glanced up, saw her, and nudged Hope, who also looked up. In the lamplight Polly saw her smile in a slightly guilty way, and shrug as if to say, What else could I do?

She drew back, closing the window, and a minute later Hope was there at the door, beckoning her into the corridor.

'Don't think badly of me,' she begged, 'but you are so good for Ruggiero I had to make sure he had you looking after him all the time.'

'So you just hi-jacked me?' Polly observed mildly.

'We will make you very welcome here,' Hope promised, avoiding a direct answer. 'You'll be paid, and of course your hotel bill has been taken care of. Please don't be angry with me.'

Her manner was placating, but it was clear that Hope Rinucci had simply taken the shortest route to getting her own way. Polly was more amused than annoyed. For one thing, moving into the villa would be helpful for her mission.

Just down the corridor she heard a door open, and the chauffeur went into the room next to Ruggiero's with her suitcase.

'I think you'll be comfortable here,' Hope said, leading her inside. 'You have only to ask for anything you want.'

After the cramped poverty of the hotel, the luxury of this room was a pleasant change. The double bed looked inviting, and there was extensive wardrobe space and a private bathroom. This was the home of a wealthy family. Ruggiero's own bedroom, though severe and reflecting a masculine taste, was furnished with the finest of everything.

Polly took a quick moment to unpack her few clothes, then changed her party outfit for jeans and flat shoes. For her top she chose a plain white blouse that she hoped would make her look nurse-like. Then she returned to Ruggiero and prepared to settle down for the night.

Hope looked in one last time, and after that the lights went off and the house grew silent. Slowly the hours ticked away, and Polly's eyelids began to droop. It had been a long day, filled with incident, and weariness was catching up with her.

Suddenly her body gave a little jerk and her eyes flew open. She breathed out hard and forced herself to wake up properly. Then she realised that Ruggiero was looking at her. She thought he was smiling faintly, but in the dark it was hard to be sure.

'All right?' he asked.

'Was I asleep long?'

'About ten minutes.'

'I'm sorry.'

'Don't apologise. It's nice to know I'm not the only one who finds things happening that weren't planned.'

He hauled himself up painfully in the bed.

'I think I ate something that disagreed with me—or drank something. Can you help me to the bathroom?'

He put an arm around her shoulder and she steadied him as far as the bathroom door, where he gingerly felt his ribs.

'You may have been right,' he conceded. 'I'm not saying you were, but you might have been. I'll manage from here.'

When he came slowly out she'd remade the bed and put on the small lamp. She reached out to help him but he waved her away.

'I'm feeling a bit more human now my stomach's settled. Ah, that's better.'

He lay down and let her pull the duvet over him.

'How's the pain?' she asked gently.

'My head isn't too bad, but my shoulder and side feel as if they've been bashed with a sledge-hammer.'

'It's time for a couple more pills. But they don't mix well with alcohol, so no more drinking until you've stopped taking them.'

'When will that be?'

'When I say,' she told him with quiet authority.

He took them from her, and accepted a glass of water, as docile now as he'd been aggressive before. When she lay back she turned out the lamp again, so that the only light in the room was the soft touch of moonlight.

'There's something different about you,' he said suddenly. 'You've changed your clothes.'

'Yes, I'm here for a few days. I've checked out of my hotel and into the room next door.'

'How did Mamma persuade you to do that?'

'Good heavens—you don't think she asked me first, do you?'

He gave a short bark of laughter that ended in a gasp of pain. 'Of course. I should have remembered Mamma's way. When did you find out?'

'When my things arrived.'

'I'm sorry. Just taking you over like that—what about your holiday?'

'That doesn't matter,' she said hastily. 'Go to sleep now.'

He stared at her for a while before saying vaguely, 'Was it you by the track?'

'Yes, it was me.'

'Are you sure? No—that's stupid—I mean—'

'Who did you think it was?' she risked saying.

'What?'

'I need to know how much you can remember. It'll tell me how serious your concussion is.'

'I did several laps and everything was all right. But then—' He took a long, shaking breath. 'Why did you come onto the track?'

'I didn't.'

'But you did. You were walking straight towards me, and your hair was blowing in the wind. I could have ridden right over you, but you didn't seem to realise that. You were smiling—like the time—'

His breathing was becoming laboured and she went to him quickly, trying to soothe him.

'It wasn't me. Truly. It was the speed that confused you, and that visor. You couldn't have seen anything properly. Just an illusion—someone who wasn't really there.'

'But—she was there,' he whispered. 'I saw her—'

'You couldn't have. It's impossible.'

'How can you be sure?'

'Because—' Suddenly realising that she was straying onto a dangerous path, she checked herself. At this moment she couldn't tell him why she was sure he would never see Sapphire again. The truth would crush him.

'Because if there had been anyone on the track you'd have hit them,' she said.

'You can't hit a ghost,' he said wearily. 'Do you believe in ghosts?'

'Yes,' she murmured, saying it almost against her will. 'I try not to, but sometimes people just won't let go—no matter what you do, they're always with you.'

'So you know that too?'

'Yes,' she said quietly. 'I know that too. Go to sleep now.'

He moved his hand forward and back, then sideways, as though searching for something. She reached out and took his hand, feeling the tension in it.

'It's going to be all right,' she said.

Some corner of his mind—the part of him that argued with everything—wanted to demand how she could be so sure. But the argument retreated before the reassurance of her clasp. His thoughts were confused.

She'd said, 'Please don't argue with me. It's a waste of time,' —talking like his mother. He'd tried to be annoyed, but it had been a relief to have her rescue him from the hole that his pride had dug for him. Hell would freeze over before he admitted that he'd been ready to collapse into bed, but she'd known without being told.

At last the tension began to fade. His eyes closed, his hand relaxed, and he was asleep.

As dawn broke Hope looked in.

'Is he all right?'

'Sleeping like a baby,' Polly assured her.

'Then why don't you go and get some sleep? I'll take over for a while.'

'Thank you.'

In her own room she snuggled blissfully down in the luxurious bed. When she awoke the sun was high in the sky. She stood under the shower, wondering what the day would bring and whether she would get the chance to fulfil her mission.

As she finished dressing she looked at her watch and was shocked to see that it was ten o'clock.

'Hope said to let you sleep,' said Evie, who'd just popped in.

'I'd better go and see my patient.'

'I'll send your breakfast up.'

She paused outside Ruggiero's room, wondering how difficult he would be this morning, and how much he would remember of the night before. She found him watching the door.

'Come in,' he said.

He sounded cautious, and she felt much the same as she approached the bed. Neither was quite sure of the other's mood, and for a moment they looked at each other.

'I apologise,' he said at last.

'For—what?'

'For whatever I did. I don't remember much about last night, but I'm pretty sure I acted unforgivably.'

'You acted like a damned fool,' she said frankly. 'Like a complete and total idiot. I've never seen such blinding stupidity in my whole life.'

'Hey, don't sit on the fence. Tell me what you really think of me.'

That broke the ice, and they shared a grin.

'Yes, I guess I shouldn't have gone clowning around after bumping my head,' he admitted. 'But, hey, it's a tough world. Don't let them see any sign of weakness or the tigers pounce.'

'But they weren't tigers at that track,' she said. 'They were your friends. And perhaps having to impress people all the time is also a sign of weakness.'

He looked alarmed. 'Are you going to psycho-analyse me?'

'That's all for today. I'll save the rest until you're feeling better.'

'I'm all right,' he said in a dispirited voice. 'Except that I don't seem to have any energy.'

'You've probably got a hangover as well as everything else. I want you to stay in bed for a while. Or are you going to fight me about that?'

'No, ma'am. I'm sure you know best.'

She regarded him cynically. 'You must be worse than I thought.'

There was no chance to say more, because Evie appeared with Polly's breakfast, and after that the rest of the family came to say goodbye before returning to their distant homes. Ruggiero greeted them all boisterously, cracked jokes and generally acted the part of a man who was on top of the world. But when it was over his forehead was damp and he was full of tension.

'That was quite a performance,' she said sympathetically.

'Sure—a sign of weakness, like you said.'

'Not this time. You sent them off easier in their minds about you.'

He tried to shrug, but immediately winced, making a face and rubbing his shoulder.

'You should let me look at that.'

She helped him off with the pyjama jacket, revealing a shoulder that looked inflamed.

'I haven't broken anything,' he said, sounding mulish again.

'Will you leave me to make the diagnosis?' she asked lightly. 'As a matter of fact I don't think you *have* broken anything, because otherwise you'd be in a lot more pain than you are. But stop trying to take over.'

'Yes, I'm wasting my time doing that with you.' He sounded resigned.

'That's right,' she told him. 'I've seen off far more troublesome patients than you.'

'Yeah?'

'Yeah!'

'*Yeah?*'

'*Yeah!*'

She was slowly working on his shoulder, feeling for injury, talking to distract him.

'On the wards they call me Nurse Bossy-Boots. People scurry for cover at my approach.'

'Think you can make me run?'

'Right this minute nothing could make you run. You might manage a stagger, but even then I'd have to hold you up.'

He started to laugh, but ended with a sharp gasp. 'Don't make me laugh,' he begged.

She eased herself behind him, one knee on the bed so that she could reach his shoulder from the best angle. He drew a deep breath of relief, muttering, 'That's better.'

For a while neither of them spoke while she worked on the shoulder, massaging it until it relaxed, then moved his arm gently in several directions. It was bruised and inflamed, but not dislocated. She finished by rubbing in some of the gel the doctor had left with her.

Studying him professionally, she saw that he was in superb physical condition, lean and muscular, as she would have expected from a man who lived an athletic life, and evenly tanned, as though he swam a good deal under the hot sun.

He carried so little weight that when he leaned forward for her to examine his spine she could easily make out its straight line, and the lines of his ribs.

'It wouldn't hurt you to gain a few pounds,' she observed, flexing her fingers gently against his skin. 'It might give you something to land on.'

'I'd put on weight if I could. I eat like a horse but I stay like this.'

'Lucky you. Lie back.'

She pressed him gently back against the pillows while she felt his ribs at the front.

'A couple of cracks,' she confirmed, 'but you've got off very lightly, considering.'

'You're not going to drag me off to hospital to be strapped up?'

'There's no need. Strapping fixes your ribs, but it can make it harder to breathe. So just be careful how you move and it'll heal naturally.'

The quiet authority in her voice seemed to ease his mind, and she felt him relaxing under her hands.

'Let's put your jacket back on,' she said. 'Then I'll give you a couple more pills.'

He winced as she slid the jacket back over his shoulders, but at last it was done. He accepted the pills with a faint smile, and was soon asleep.

The house was quiet now that the guests had departed, and Hope, Toni and Francesco had travelled to the airport to see off the English party. Polly listened to the silence, which seemed to have an edgy quality, and thought she was being warned that this tranquil time could not last for ever. The moment was approaching.

She slipped next door and found the picture of Freda and the young man she now knew as Ruggiero. She studied his face a while, trying to reconcile its glowing joy with the dour, tense individual he had become. Then she put it in her pocket and returned to sit quietly with him until she heard a car return late in the afternoon.

Hope and Toni came in together, full of gratitude.

'I will stay with my son for a while,' Toni said, 'while you go down for supper.'

Ruggiero was awake but drowsy as Toni slipped into the room.

'All gone?' he asked, yawning.

'Their flight took off on time. How are you feeling?'

'OK, I guess. I seem to be floating.' Suddenly he remembered. 'Poppa, do you know what Mamma did? She practically kidnapped Polly.'

'Don't blame me,' his father said hastily. 'I knew nothing about it until it was too late. You know your mother.'

'But didn't you make some protest?'

'Why? I'm glad you're being properly cared for.'

'I guess she told you what to say,' Ruggiero

said with wry amusement. 'You're bullied—you know that?'

'Oh, no,' Toni said seriously. 'Your *mamma* never bullies me. She knows what I need before I know myself, and she makes sure that I have it.'

'There's a difference?'

'Yes,' Toni said simply. 'There's a difference.'

Downstairs the table was spread with a banquet, and Polly found herself treated as an honoured guest. Hope ceremonially poured champagne, clinked glasses, and produced an envelope plump with euros.

'But this is far too much,' Polly gasped. 'I can't take it all.'

'You are worth every penny,' Hope declared. 'Not only for what you are doing for us, but also because you have allowed us to take over your holiday without complaint.'

'That's all right,' Polly said awkwardly. 'It wasn't really a holiday.'

'Do you mean that you have to return to England soon? When are you due back at your job?'

'I don't have a job at the moment.'

'Aha—then you are free to remain as long as you wish. Good. You will stay with us. Now, let us eat.'

Toni joined them after a while, with the news that Ruggiero was sleeping.

'I'll go back fairly soon,' Polly said.

They made it hard for her—treating her like a queen, toasting her with champagne, encouraging her to talk about herself. That was a dangerous subject, and she had to be circumspect, but these were warm-hearted people, taking what they wanted with a charm that threatened to melt her heart.

As soon as possible she brought the conversation back to Ruggiero, explaining about his condition and how she could take care of it.

'He'll be fine if he can be persuaded to rest for a few days,' she finished.

'You can persuade him,' Hope declared. 'You have him eating out of your hand.'

Polly put her head on one side. 'I try to picture him eating out of anyone's hand,' she said whimsically, 'but it's beyond me.' As they laughed, she added, 'Thank you for a lovely meal. Now I think I'll go upstairs and crack the whip a little. Goodnight.'

She seated herself quietly beside Ruggiero's bed, seeing with satisfaction that he was deeply, contentedly asleep. She waited beside him for a while, dozing gently herself, so that she didn't notice when he awoke, and didn't know that his eyes were open until he murmured, 'Polly.'

'Yes, I'm here. Is something the matter?'

'Yes, in a way. I'm so sorry.'

'Hey, you've already apologised.'

'For being a jerk, but not for—' He broke off, groaning, 'I hit you, didn't I? When you were by me on the track—I seem to remember—'

'You sent me flying,' she said lightly. 'But it was an accident. You didn't mean to do it. You were just flailing around blindly.'

'I do a lot of that, I'm afraid.'

'It wasn't your fault,' she said in a rallying voice. 'Why are you so determined to give yourself a hard time?'

'Perhaps somebody ought to,' he said grimly.

She was touched by this glimpse of humility, so unexpected.

'You're very quiet,' he said. 'Are you sure you don't blame me?'

'Honestly—it's not that.'

'Then what is it? What's the mystery, Polly? And don't try to brush me off, because I've been lying here doing a lot of thinking, and I don't reckon you just happened to be at the track—did you?'

'No,' she admitted. 'It wasn't an accident.' She took a long breath. 'Maybe it's time I told you everything.'

Suddenly the enormity of what she had to tell him came over her. She'd wanted to choose her moment—not have it forced on her like this.

'I meant to tell you earlier,' she said at last. 'But then you were ill so I had to wait.'

'Whatever it is, I think I need to know.'

Switching on the bedside lamp, she reached into her bag and took out the photograph of him with Freda.

'I think this will explain part of it,' she said, handing it to him.

As he stared at the picture she saw a change come over him—but not the one she'd expected. After the first shock he became possessed by dark fury.

'You've been going through my things,' he accused.

'Of course not.'

'You must have done, or you couldn't have this picture.'

'That isn't yours,' she said urgently.

'Don't lie to me.'

'I'm not lying. I have one too. Yours is still wherever you keep it.'

He hauled himself up in bed, wincing, so that she reached out to help him. He pushed her away.

'Get off me,' he snapped.

She realised that she should have thought of this, but she hadn't.

He made it painfully over to the chest of drawers on the far side of the room, pulled open the top drawer and reached deep inside. Polly wondered at the swift change in him. There was no trace now of the humility that had briefly touched her heart. His streak of ferocity, never far below the surface, had reasserted itself.

She saw his face change as he drew something out of the drawer and looked at it. She guessed it was the companion picture. Coming slowly back to the bed, he almost fell onto it, breathing hard with the pain. In silence she handed the first photograph back to him. He gazed from one picture to the other, like a man who'd received a stunning blow.

'Where did you get this?' he demanded hoarsely.

'She gave it to me.'

'She?'

'My cousin—Freda. She said you went to the funfair together and had the pictures taken in a machine. There were two, and you took one each.'

'Freda?'

'You knew her as Sapphire.'

He turned his head on the pillow, looking at her intently.

'Take your hair down,' he said.

'Surely there's—?'

'Do it.'

A quick movement and it fell about her face. She guessed that the dim light emphasised her likeness to Freda, and was certain of it when he closed his eyes, as if to shut her out.

'That's why I thought you were her,' he said, almost to himself.

'It's not much of a resemblance. She was always the beautiful one.'

He opened his eyes again and studied her. She was sure the contrast between her and his fantasy image struck painfully.

'You said she's your cousin?'

'She *was*,' Polly said softly. 'She's dead now.'

CHAPTER FOUR

'DEAD,' he whispered. 'No—you didn't say that. I just thought for a moment—'

'She's dead,' Polly repeated softly. 'A few weeks ago.'

He looked away, concealing his face from her, while his fingers moved compulsively on the photograph until it began to crumple.

'Go on,' he said at last, in a voice that seemed to come from a great distance.

'Her real name was Freda Hanson—until she married George Ranley, six years ago.'

He stirred. 'She was married when I knew her?'

'Yes.'

'He made her unhappy? She no longer loved him?'

'I don't think she was ever madly in love with him,' Polly said, choosing her words carefully. 'He's very rich, and—'

'Stop there,' he said quickly. 'If you're trying to

tell me that she married for money—don't. She wouldn't—not the girl I knew.'

'But you *didn't* know her,' Polly said gently. 'Don't you realise that she made sure of that? She didn't even tell you her real name. That way you couldn't find her again when she went home.'

'Where was home?'

'In Yorkshire, in the north of England.'

'How much do you know of what happened between her and me?'

'You met in a bar in a London hotel, and you were together for two weeks.'

'You could put it like that,' he said slowly. 'But the truth was so much more. What we had was there from the first moment. I looked at her, and I wanted her so badly that I was afraid it must show. I even thought I might scare her off. But nothing frightened her. She was brave. She went out to meet life—she came to me at once.'

There was an aching wistfulness in his voice that saddened Polly. She knew the truth behind her cousin's 'bravery'. She hadn't had much time to pursue her object. That was the ugly fact, and it was painful to see this blunt, forceful man reduced to misery by her ruthless tactics.

'I remember being surprised that she was English,' Ruggiero continued. 'I thought English women were prim and proper. But not her. She loved me as though I was the only man on earth.'

'Didn't you think it strange that she wouldn't tell you her full name?'

'At the time it almost seemed irrelevant—something that could be sorted out later. What she gave me—I'm not good with words, I couldn't describe it—but it made me a different man. Better.'

There was something almost shocking in the quiet simplicity of the last word. Hesitantly, Polly asked, 'How do you mean, better?'

Slowly he laid his fingers over his heart.

'What's in here has always been just for me,' he said. 'I've kept it that way. A man's safer that way.'

'But why must he always be safe?' she ventured to ask.

'That's what she made me ask myself. It was like becoming someone else—ready to take risks I couldn't take before, glad of it. I even enjoyed her laughing at me. I've never found it easy to be laughed at, but she—well, I'd have accepted anything from her.'

Against her will Polly heard Freda's voice in her head, chuckling.

'The tougher they are, the more fun it is when they become my slaves.'

And this was the result—this bleak, desolate

man holding onto his belief in her like a drowning man clinging to a raft. What would become of him in a few moments when that comfort was finally snatched away?

'What happened after she left me?' he asked.

Polly took a deep breath.

'She went back to George, and nine months later she had a baby.'

He stared at her. 'Are you saying—?'

'*Your* baby.'

He hauled himself up again, waving her away so that he could sit on the edge of the bed, his back to her.

'How can you be sure it's mine?' he demanded harshly.

'It isn't George's. It couldn't be.'

'But why didn't she tell me? I never concealed where I lived. Why didn't she come to me? She couldn't have thought I'd turn my back on her. She knew how much I— She knew—'

'She didn't want you told.'

'But—'

'She wanted to stay married to George, so she had an affair hoping to get pregnant.'

For a moment he was as still as if he'd been punched over the heart.

'Shut up!' he said at last in a fierce voice. 'Do you know what you're saying about her?'

'Yes,' she said, with a touch of sadness. 'I'm saying that she planned everything.'

'You're saying she was a calculating, cold-hearted bitch?'

'No, I'm not,' she insisted. 'She could be warm and funny and generous. But when she came to London that time she wanted something, and it turned out to be you.'

'You don't know what you're talking about,' he snapped. 'You don't know how it was with us when we were together—how could you understand—?'

She remembered George when he'd learned the truth, wailing pitiably, 'I thought she really loved me.'

The mood hadn't lasted. He'd become vicious and vengeful, but she'd briefly glimpsed the devastation that Freda could cause. She'd been a genius at inspiring love by pretending love, and she'd obviously done it well with both men.

'Did her husband think the child was his?' Ruggiero asked.

'At first, yes. Then he found out by chance that he had a very low sperm count, and he began to doubt. He demanded a test, and when he discovered that he wasn't the father he threw Freda and the baby out of the house.'

'When was this?'

'Almost a year ago.'

'Why didn't she come to me then?'

Because she'd hoped to entice George back, was the truthful answer. But Polly couldn't bring herself to hurt him more, so she softened it.

'She was already growing thin from illness. She said she'd contact you when she got well. But she never did. She came to live with me. I nursed her as best I could, but it was hopeless. She made me promise to find you afterwards—to tell you that you have a son.'

'She's dead,' he murmured. 'Dead—and I wasn't with her.'

In the face of his pain there was nothing she could say.

'Why didn't I know?' he demanded. 'How come I didn't sense it when we were so close?'

Polly was silent, knowing that Freda had never felt close to him.

'You should have found a way to contact me while she was alive,' he insisted.

'I couldn't. She wouldn't tell me where to find you. I didn't even know that you lived in Naples. I found out that and the name of this villa in a letter she wrote me, to be opened when she was dead.'

'I would have looked after her,' he said in a daze.

'She didn't want you to see her. She hated not being beautiful any more.'

'Do you think I'd have cared about that?' he flashed, with a hint of ferocity. 'I wouldn't even have seen it. I *lo*—'

He stopped himself with a sharp breath, like a man pulling back from the brink. His haggard eyes met hers.

'It's too late,' he said, like a man facing the bleak truth for the first time. 'Too late.'

'I'm sorry,' she whispered. She reached for him but he flinched away.

'I want you to go,' he said.

'But—'

'Get out, for pity's sake!' he said in agony.

She rose, reaching out for her copy of the picture, but he took it, saying curtly, 'Leave that.'

At the door she glanced back at him. He was holding both pictures, looking from one to the other as though in this way he might discover a secret. He didn't notice as she left.

Polly understood his need to be alone. She shared it. The conversation had been even harder than she'd expected. She'd been fooled by Freda's 'love-'em-and-leave-'em' description of Ruggiero, thinking he might take the news in that spirit.

Instead, his explosion of emotion had astonished her. Suddenly she saw the chasm yawning at her feet. From the first moment everything about Ruggiero had been a surprise—starting with the discovery that her cousin haunted him. She should have been prepared for tonight, but she'd sensed the danger almost too late.

'You're saying she was a calculating, cold-hearted bitch?'

He'd spoken as though the mere thought was outrageous, but it was an exact description of Freda. In the great days of her beauty she would have taken it as a compliment.

'It's such fun to make them sit up and beg,' she'd once trilled. 'You can make a man do anything if you go about it the right way.'

Later, talking about Ruggiero, with his baby in her arms, she'd said, 'He was the best—know what I mean? Well, no—maybe you don't.'

'I certainly don't have your wide experience for making comparisons,' Polly had replied, trying to speak lightly.

'Well, take my word for it. Ruggiero was really something in bed.' She had given a luxurious gurgle. 'Every woman should have an Italian lover. There are things about passion that only they understand.'

There had been no affection in her voice. Freda had taken what she wanted from her lover, then dispensed with him. She'd appreciated his technical skills, but she'd never thought of him as a person.

And in that she'd lost out, Polly realised. Clever as she was, Freda hadn't discovered the things that made Ruggiero truly fascinating: the contrast between the contrived self that he showed to the world and the true self that he hid as though alarmed by it, the mulish stubbornness that collapsed into unexpected moments of self-deprecating humour. He was intriguing because everything about him contradicted everything else. A woman could spend years trying to understand him, enjoying every moment of the challenge, and Freda hadn't suspected it.

I've seen it, Polly thought suddenly. But I didn't want to. Heaven help me, this is no time to be falling into that trap! I'm just here to do a job.

She'd been clumsy tonight—hinting that his goddess had had feet of clay, which he hadn't been ready to hear. He'd loved Sapphire, perhaps without fully realising it until that moment. If so, it was a cruel discovery made in the cruellest possible way.

She'd wanted to escape him before—but now she wanted to be with him, consoling him.

She went out into the corridor, pausing outside his door, her hand raised to knock. But then she heard a soft, rhythmic sound coming from inside the room, as though a man was thumping the wall in rage and misery.

She turned away.

Polly spent the rest of the night sitting up by the window, thinking of him, alone in his suffering, because that was how he preferred it. The thought of that appalling bleakness made her shudder, and her heart reached out to him. But she wasn't the one he wanted.

At last, as dawn began to break, there was a soft knock at her door. He was standing there, a cotton robe over his pyjamas. The anger had gone from his face, leaving only weariness.

'Come in,' she said quietly.

But he didn't move, only looked at her with a kind of desperation.

'What is it?' she asked. 'Can't I help you?'

'I'm not sure—perhaps I should—'

'Why don't you come in and talk about it?'

He looked at her, feeling himself paralysed by indecision. His self-confidence had drained away without warning, and now he hardly knew how to cope.

He'd dismissed Polly from his sight, but even then he'd known that he must follow her. He resented her, almost hated her, but against his will he was drawn after her. Now he stood on her threshold, fighting an impulse to back off, knowing that if he yielded to it a deep need would make him return.

'Let's talk,' she said gently, taking his arm and drawing him inside.

He sat uneasily on the bed.

'I seem to have a mountain of apologies to make.'

'Never mind,' she told him lightly. 'You've had a big shock.'

'I shouldn't have taken it out on you.'

'It's over. Past. Forget it.'

'Thank you. Polly, did I imagine that whole mad conversation? Did you tell me that Sapphire was dead and I have a son?'

'Yes.'

'And that's why you're here? It wasn't chance that we met?'

'No, I knew you lived in Naples, and I knew about this villa. I'd have come here first, but there was something in the newspaper about your brother's wedding. It mentioned your firm, so I went there and found out about the racetrack. Ruggiero, please believe me—I haven't been spying on you. I stayed here because it gave me a chance to be near you and choose my moment. I wanted to explain before, but you were ill—how could I?'

She made a helpless gesture, and he nodded.

'OK, I understand that. Although it gives me an awkward feeling to remember the curious looks I've seen you giving me.'

'I was a nurse, studying a patient for signs of trouble.'

'And maybe you were also remembering things Sapphire said about me and thinking, *Him?*'

He said the last word with a searing irony that took her breath away.

'I was curious about little Matthew's father,' she said cautiously. 'This last year I've got to love him very much. I can't wait to show him to you.'

His answer shattered her.

'I don't want to see him.'

'What?'

'I want nothing to do with him,' he growled. 'Why didn't you leave well alone?'

'Because Matthew is your son, and he needs a family.'

'He has you.'

'I'm not his parent. You are. Don't you even want to *see* him?'

'Is there any reason why I should?' he asked, almost brutally.

'A few hours ago you were saying I should have come here sooner.'

'Yes, when *she* was alive. I could have been with her. But this child is a stranger. I can't feel it's part of me.'

'He was part of *her*,' Polly said quietly. 'Doesn't that mean anything?'

'It might have done if she'd wanted me to know about it.'

'Will you stop talking about "it"?' Polly demanded, becoming annoyed. 'Matthew is a he. He's a baby. He needs love and care—'

'If he's mine, I'll support him.'

'Money?' she snapped. 'Do you really think that's all there is to being a father?'

'I don't feel like a father. This is the best I can do.'

'Then it's not good enough,' she retorted.

'Do you think a father's love can be turned on and off at the press of a switch?' he demanded, equally angry. 'Or any other kind of love?'

'No, of course it can't. But you can turn the love you used to feel to account now. You can't give your love to her, so give it to the child you share.'

'Share? Did she share him with me? If she hadn't died I'd have known nothing.'

'But she did die, so why not be gentle with her memory? She can't hurt you now.'

'Can't—?' He stared at her in sheer outrage before saying, with soft vehemence, 'The dead can hurt you more than the living, because things can't be put right. You can't go back and explain, or apologise, or say the healing words, and the wounds stay open for ever. How can I be gentle with her memory when what she did to me will never end?'

'She gave you a child,' Polly said. 'Whatever she intended, that's what happened. Matthew's alive, and he carries part of you in him.'

He didn't answer for a while, but at last he said, 'Who does he look like?'

She took out a picture and handed it to him. It showed a toddler of eighteen months, with Ruggiero's colouring, dark, sparkling eyes and a brilliant smile.

How could anyone resist this little charmer? she thought. But after a glance he handed it back.

'I can't take him,' he said. 'But of course I'll support him—and I'll support you while you care for him.'

'Excuse me—I'm not looking for a job as a hired nanny.'

'I didn't mean it like that. It wouldn't just be wages; it would be a generous income. You could live comfortably.'

'Oh, really? So you think using cash to avoid your responsibilities is fine as long as the gesture is big enough?'

'I didn't mean—Look, he already knows you. He'd probably rather stay with you.'

'And how about what *I'd* rather? I'm a trained nurse, and I'd like to starting working again.'

She was making it up as she went along. She adored little Matthew, and part of her longed to keep him. If she hadn't liked what she found in Naples she would have left without revealing his existence.

But she did like it. The Rinuccis fitted her inner picture of the perfect family—riotous and colourful, with plenty of love and laughter to go around.

Ruggiero himself would need a little work to improve him, she thought, but in the meantime she would entrust Matthew to Hope and Toni without a qualm. And with all those uncles, aunts and cousins life would be happier for the little boy than in the narrow existence he would find with her.

'How can you reject him?' she demanded, indicating the picture. 'He's your flesh and blood.'

'For Pete's sake,' he snapped. 'You spring this on me and expect me to press a button and have all the right reactions. Just what *is* the right reaction to a son I never knew I had from a woman who didn't even tell me her real name?'

'Don't you feel anything for him?'

'No,' he said after a moment. 'Nothing.'

It wasn't true, she guessed. He was in pain. In trying to numb that, he had numbed every other feeling.

'I'd like you to think about keeping him,' he said. 'On the terms we discussed.'

'We did not discuss anything,' she said, her temper mounting again. 'You laid down your requirements and expected me to fall into line.'

'Just think about it.'

'No!'

'Why the hell not?'

'Because my fiancé would never agree.'

'What?'

'The man I'm engaged to marry doesn't want a child that isn't ours,' she said deliberately.

'You didn't mention an engagement before.'

'There was no need. It's no concern of yours. I came here because little Matthew has a right to his family, but when I've seen him settled I'm returning to my own life.'

He rose. 'I'm going. I need to think about this.'

He moved swiftly towards the door, but when he'd opened it he halted, transfixed.

'Good morning,' said a sweet voice.

Hope was standing there in her dressing gown.

'Mamma, what are you doing here?'

'I came to see why you two are making so much noise. Normally, of course, I wouldn't enquire. It would be indelicate—'

'Mamma!'

'Don't be a prude, my son. It doesn't suit you. Polly, please tell me what has happened.'

'I think Ruggiero had better tell you.'

'If one of you doesn't tell me something soon I shall get cross.'

Ruggiero handed her the picture of Matthew.

'I knew his mother briefly a little more than two years ago in England,' he said, in a flat voice, blank of emotion. 'She never told me about him. Now she's dead.'

'She was my cousin,' Polly supplied. 'She wanted me to find Ruggiero after her death and tell him about his son.'

To her relief, Hope asked no awkward questions. She was entranced by the picture.

'This little man is my grandson?' she asked, in tones of wonder.

Polly gave the exact date of Matthew's birth, and Ruggiero nodded.

'Nine months,' he said briefly.

Hope's eyes were alight with fondness, just as Polly had hoped.

'Such a little darling,' she murmured. 'Where is he now?'

'In England,' Polly told her. 'Some friends of mine are caring for him while I'm here.'

'How soon can we fetch him?'

'*Mamma!*'

'Your son no longer has a mother, but he has a father. Of course he belongs here.'

'I think so too,' Polly said. 'I believe he's a Rinucci. But of course it can be easily established with a test.'

Hope pulled a face. 'No need. If he's one of us

I'll know as soon as I hold him in my arms. I'll book the flight to England at once. Polly, you will return here with me, won't you? To help him settle in.'

'Her fiancé may object,' Ruggiero observed.

'He won't,' Polly said hastily. 'Yes, I'll come back for a while.'

Hope cast her a strange look, but said nothing. Wasting no time, she picked up Polly's bedside phone, called the airport, and found a flight to London that afternoon.

By now the light was growing, and the house was waking up around them. Hope bustled away to tell everyone of the plan for today.

'I'm afraid you got taken over again,' Ruggiero said wryly.

'That's all right. I'm glad about this. Hope will love him—'

'Even if I don't? Is that what you mean?'

'You will—in the end. Perhaps you should go now.'

It was a relief when he left. She needed time to work out more details of her 'fiancé'.

He's a doctor called Brian, she decided. And I met him at the hospital where I used to work. And he's doing a lot of night shifts, so he's hard to get hold of.

She'd invented a fiancé on the spur of the moment, solely to silence Ruggiero in their argument. If she'd stopped to consider first she might not have done it.

But that's me, she thought ruefully. Speak first, think afterwards. I might have come up with something else if I'd had time, or if Ruggiero couldn't annoy me so much that—ah, well. I'm stuck with a 'fiancé' now, so I may as well make use of him.

Today Ruggiero went downstairs for breakfast. Polly found herself sitting next to Toni, who seemed eager to talk to her. She'd seen little of him before, but now she found him a gentle, soft-spoken man, full of joy about his new grandson.

'You won't stay away too long, will you?' he asked anxiously.

'That's up to Hope,' she said. 'She's arranging everything.'

For a moment his eyes rested fondly on his wife.

'Yes,' he said. 'She knows just how to make everything right.'

After breakfast she called the friends caring for Matthew to say she was on her way. Then she went looking for Ruggiero, and found him in the garden, sitting on a fallen log, looking at his clasped hands.

'I've left you some of those pills, but use them sparingly,' she said.

'I probably won't need them. I feel better now I'm up.'

'Good. But don't overdo it.' A sudden suspicion made her add, '*Don't* go back to work.'

'I'll just drop in to talk to my partner. No racing, I promise.'

'Your partner can visit you here.'

'And let him see me looking like an invalid? Forget it.'

'Is there any way to get some sense into you?'

'Nope, so stop wasting your time.'

There was a sulphurous silence. Then he grinned reluctantly.

'Sorry if I give you a hard time.'

But she had his measure by now. 'You're not sorry. That ritual apology is just to shut me up.'

'Well, it's failed, hasn't it? As a matter of interest, has anyone ever actually managed to shut you up?'

'Would I tell you?'

'Not if you were wise.' He grinned again, more warmly this time. 'I promise to be good while you're gone.'

He brightened suddenly.

'You and my mother have a lot in common. The way you took your fiancé's consent for granted was very like her. What's his name, by the way?'

'Brian,' she said quickly. 'And he'll understand about my coming back here. After all, it won't be for long.'

'What did he say when you called to tell him?'

'I haven't done that yet.'

'You'd better hurry if you want him to meet you at the airport.'

'He can't. He's a hospital doctor and he's on night duty at the moment,' she said, repeating the story she'd mapped out. 'I'd better go and get ready.'

Before she could move he reached out and took her hand.

'A moment,' he said. 'I want to ask you a favour.'

But he stopped there, as though it was hard for him to go on.

'What can I do for you?' she asked gently.

His hand tightened on hers.

'When you get home—do you have any more pictures of her?'

'Yes, I have plenty. I'll bring some of them to you.'

'Bring them all. Everything—*please.*'

'There are a lot of blanks to be filled in, aren't there?'

'I used to think I'd have the chance to fill them in one day. I never thought it would be like this, when it's too late to make any difference.'

But it could still make a difference, she thought. It would help him learn to relate to his son, and she would do everything in her power to help that happen.

'You'd better let me go,' she said, wincing slightly.

He seemed to return from a distance, to realise that he was gripping her hand hard. He made an exclamation as he released it and began to rub it between his two hands.

'I think the circulation's started again now,' she said lightly.

'I'm sorry—again. Hell! Why don't I just give you a big apology now, and hopefully it'll cover everything in the future?'

'Well, I'm leaving in a couple of hours,' she said lightly. 'You won't have time to annoy me before then.'

'You underestimate me. Let's go in.'

He helped her to her feet and they walked indoors, briefly in accord.

CHAPTER FIVE

THEY were to spend two nights in England—the first in Polly's home and the second with Justin and Evie, who were eager to see the new arrival.

During the flight Hope asked about Polly's fiancé, assuming, as Ruggiero had done, that he would meet them. Polly repeated the excuse about 'Brian's' night duty, and Hope seemed to accept it.

Although the matriarch of an Italian family, Hope was English, and she knew the country well.

'How do you come to live in London if you come from Yorkshire?' she asked.

'I was engaged several years ago, but we broke up. I wanted to get away so I came south. Freda joined me when she became ill.'

'And the baby is—how old?'

'Eighteen months.'

'Is he walking?'

'Oh, yes, he's well grown. He took his first tentative step at nine months.'

'So did Ruggiero,' Hope said with satisfaction. 'He and Carlo competed to see who could walk first, and they've been vying with each other ever since.'

They were to collect Matthew the next morning, as it would be too late to do it that day. The light was fading when they arrived in the evening. When they had sent out for a take-away meal, and were sitting together in the tiny kitchen, Hope said gently, 'Why don't you tell me the things you couldn't say in front of Ruggiero?'

Faced with this kindly understanding, Polly explained everything. At the end Hope nodded sadly.

'He said very little when he got home—something about a "holiday romance", but so casually that it seemed to mean nothing. I should have seen through that, but there had been so many—' She made a sad gesture.

'I imagine he was very determined to keep his secrets?' Polly suggested. 'Freda summed him up as "love 'em and leave 'em," and maybe for a man like that…' She hesitated, but Hope understood.

'It would be very difficult to find that he was the one left,' she filled in. 'That must have made it harder for him to cope with. I wonder how much more there was?'

'I don't know—and I'm sure he doesn't,' Polly reflected. 'It was all built on fantasies, because he knew nothing about her—not that she was married, or that she had a secret agenda. He didn't even know her real name. I know how you must feel about her, but please don't hate her.'

'Once I might have done,' Hope admitted. 'But she ended so sadly that I must forgive her. Is this where you lived together?'

'Yes, until just a few weeks ago. Then she went into hospital for the last time.'

'She was beautiful,' Hope said, studying the pictures.

'It was more than just beauty. She had that extra "something" that we'd all like to have. A kind of magic. I think he's been trying to cope by pretending to himself that that it really was just a holiday romance. He might have managed it if I hadn't turned up. Now he has to face what actually happened, and I don't think he knows how.'

'But you'll help him, won't you?' Hope urged. 'You are special to him because of her. You're the only one he can turn to now. I, his mother, say so.'

'I'll do my best. I want things to turn out well for little Matthew.'

'And only for him? Oh, yes—you are engaged to be married, aren't you? I forgot.'

When they had gone to bed Polly lay awake, feeling the little flat full of ghosts. Freda seemed to be here again, chattering feverishly about herself and her conquests, especially Ruggiero.

'He was so strong, Polly, and that makes a man so much more exciting. He'd hold me tight in his arms and love me and love me and love me, all through the night. But he always had energy for more.'

By then her sickness had been far advanced, her beauty gone, and Polly had listened kindly to the tales of triumphs that would never come again.

'He's an athlete, you know,' Freda had purred. 'Likes to live an active life. Well, I could see that as soon as he was naked—all well-developed muscles and not an ounce of fat. Just looking at him, I knew he was made for love.' Then she'd given Polly a sideways glance, with a touch of malice. 'I don't disturb you, talking like that, do I?'

'No,' Polly had said. 'You don't.'

It was true. In those days Ruggiero had had no reality for her. Freda's descriptions had conjured up no pictures.

But things had changed. Now that she'd seen him and held him in her arms the words came alive with vivid meaning.

'I knew he was made for love.'

She sat up sharply, breathing hard, staring into the darkness.

'Nonsense,' she said to herself.

Suddenly it was impossible to sleep. She had to get up and walk restlessly about.

'It's getting to me,' she muttered. 'I need to finish this, come home, get a job, live a normal life—whatever that is—and forget about him.'

It was impossible. She could vividly recall running her fingers over his skin, seeking injuries; a coolly professional action at the time, but one which brought her senses alive in retrospect.

But what affected her even more was the memory of him clasping her hand with painful intensity as he begged for some pictures of the woman he'd loved, and spoke the terrible words 'too late'.

In her mind she heard Hope saying, 'You are special to him,' and was dismayed at the tiny flicker of pleasure she'd felt until Hope had quenched it by adding, 'because of her.'

Special to him, but only because of her, she thought. I guess I'd better remember that, just in case I get any silly ideas.

She lay down again, and, by dint of talking sensibly to herself, finally managed to get to sleep.

Next morning was chaos. Iris, the friend caring for Matthew, called early to say that one of her own children was being whisked to hospital with a broken leg, and she needed to off-load the baby fast.

'Joe will pass your house on the way to the hospital.'

Joe, her husband, turned up half an hour later with Matthew. The toddler, sensing a crisis, was bawling at the top of his voice, drowning out Polly's attempts to introduce Hope, enquire after the injured daughter, and thank him.

Luckily Hope knew all about babies, and picked him up without the slightest fuss or bother. Polly had thought of so many things to say, but nothing was necessary. Hope cooed and smiled—until the noise died suddenly, and grandson and grandmother were left considering each other in silence.

He burped.

A broad smile broke over Hope's face and she laughed in delight. At once he returned the smile, burping again. Hope pulled him tightly against her and dropped her head so that her face was hidden. When she raised it again there were tears on her cheeks.

'My grandson,' she said huskily. 'Oh, yes, he's mine. We knew each other at once.'

As they got ready to leave Hope said, 'Why don't you call your fiancé and invite him to join us tonight at Justin and Evie's place?'

'That's kind of you,' Polly said hastily. 'But I don't think he could get away—'

'But you won't know if you don't ask him. Or you could slip out and see him now. We have a few extra hours, since Matthew is here early, so you could make use of them.'

Polly assented, because she guessed her refusals might start to sound unconvincing. It would give her a couple of hours to do some shopping.

'Have you had a good time?' Hope asked as soon as she arrived home.

'Wonderful, thank you,' she said brightly.

She just about managed to infuse her manner with delight, as befitted a woman who'd seized a few stolen minutes with her lover, but she wasn't enough of an actress to carry it further, so when Hope would ask more questions she gave a little shriek.

'Is that the time? We should be going or we'll be late.'

Soon they were on their way to Justin and Evie's home, and mercifully Hope dropped the subject. She talked instead about the phone call she'd had with Ruggiero.

'I told him all about his son, how beautiful he is. I said you were out so little Matthew and I were getting to know each other. He sounded very pleased.'

Polly longed to ask if Hope had told Ruggiero that she was meeting Brian, but she didn't dare. Instead she said how much she was looking forward to talking to Evie again, and soon they reached their destination.

After the tense misery of the last year it was wonderful to visit a cheerful home, with a husband and wife who loved each other, their baby twins, and Justin's teenage son. Evie and Hope went into a happy huddle over Matthew, who was all smiles for a while, but then tried to play a rough game with the family puppy, who objected and ran away. The toddler vented his frustration in a screaming fit.

'Just like his father,' Hope observed, picking him up. 'He always roared at the world when it didn't dance to his tune.'

Her eyes met Polly's and the silent message, *And he hasn't changed*, flashed between them.

'You two really understand each other,' Evie said when she and Hope were alone. 'Have you decided on her?'

'I don't know what you mean,' Hope said with an air of innocence.

'Oh, yes, you do,' Evie chuckled. 'You pick out a daughter-in-law and pull strings until you get her.'

'I merely like to ensure the best for my sons,' Hope said.

'And you've decided on Polly. Go on, admit it.'

'She might be the making of him,' Hope agreed. 'But we have to go carefully.'

'Yes, her fiancé might get in the way a little.'

'I don't think so,' Hope mused. 'No, I really don't think so at all.'

They flew back to Italy the next day. Polly spent the last half hour looking out of the plane window, trying to understand the sudden nervousness that had come over her.

Ruggiero was in her thoughts all the time, but he'd been at a safe distance. Now she would be with him again, and the awareness that had come to her so suddenly, two nights ago, was disturbing her. She wasn't sure what to think, but she'd know when she saw him.

It was just fancy, she tried to reassure herself. I'm a severely practical person. This sort of thing just doesn't happen to me, because I don't let it. I wonder if he'll be at the airport?

He was. He and Toni stood there, waiting as they came out of Customs, Hope carrying the child, and Polly saw Toni's face light up with joy. Then he was running forward, arms outstretched, to embrace his wife and grandson together.

Ruggiero's face remained blank. Nor did he move as Toni and Polly greeted each other pleasantly.

'All this has thrown him for six,' Toni muttered in her ear. 'Since my wife called he hasn't known what to do with himself.'

That could be taken both ways, she thought. It didn't tell her about Ruggiero's true feelings. But then she saw him smiling at her with a hint of relief, as though he'd just been hanging on until she came back. And, despite her efforts to stop it, a spring of pleasure welled up inside her.

They had come in two cars, to ensure enough room for everyone on the return journey.

'You and the baby go with Poppa,' Ruggiero told his mother. 'I'll take Polly.'

The little surge of happiness was there again, irrational and reprehensible, but too strong to be fought. He opened the door for her and made sure she was comfortable before going around to the driver's side. She looked at him, smiling. She couldn't help herself. Something told her that his next words would be momentous.

As Toni's car pulled away Ruggiero turned to her.

'Let them go for the moment,' he said. 'There is something I must say to you first.'

'Yes?'

'You did bring them, didn't you?'

'What?'

'The pictures. You promised faithfully to bring me pictures of Sapphire. Please, Polly, don't tell me you forgot. You don't know how important it is.'

So this was all he wanted—why he'd lit up at

the sight of her. The depth of her bitterness warned her how far she'd strayed into danger.

'Please, Polly,' he repeated.

'It's all right. I've brought the pictures.'

With sudden resolution, as though he'd been given a reviving draught of life, he started the car and swung out of the airport.

Well, what did you think was going to happen? Polly thought scathingly. That he was going to forget her and see you? Get real!

On the way home she said, 'Have you been sensible while I was away?'

'No riding. I swear it.'

'Short of that.'

'I dropped in at work for an hour, but I behaved very feebly, and came home early. You'd have been proud of me.'

'How about the pills?'

'Just a couple at night. I'm on the mend.'

When they reached the villa Primo and Olympia were there. Apart from Carlo and Della, away on their honeymoon, they were the only Rinuccis who lived in Naples, so their arrival represented the rest of the family.

At first Polly stayed where Matthew could always see her, lest he grow alarmed. But he was easy in company—a natural charmer, who relished the attention.

Everyone was delighted when Ruggiero dropped down on one knee to look his son in the eye, and received a steady stare in return.

'*Buongiorno,*' Ruggiero said politely.

'*Bon—bon—*' he tried to repeat.

Ruggiero repeated the word and the tot responded by yelling, '*Bon, bon, bon!*' in tones of delight.

Everyone laughed and clapped.

'His first Italian word,' Hope cried. 'Why don't you sit down and hold him?'

He sat on the sofa, and she helped little Matthew to get up beside him. He peered closely at this new giant, and finally became curious enough to try to climb onto his lap.

'Better not,' Ruggiero said quickly. 'I'm still a bit sore, and I'd be afraid of dropping him.'

It was an entirely reasonable excuse. Surely Polly only imagined that he'd seized the first chance to back off?

He behaved impeccably, regarding the child with apparent interest, smiling in the right places, watching as he was bathed and dressed in the sleepsuit that Polly had brought with her, then put to bed. It was agreed, for the moment, that he should sleep in Polly's room, in a crib that one of the maids had rescued from the attic.

'I suppose you're going to say that was mine?' Ruggiero asked with resigned good humour.

'No, this was Carlo's,' Hope declared triumphantly. 'You managed to set fire to yours.'

Everyone laughed, including Ruggiero, but it seemed to Polly that he was doing everything from a distance, trying not to reveal that this first meeting with his son meant nothing to him.

When Matthew had fallen asleep, Ruggiero said unexpectedly, 'Could you all give us a moment, please?'

Everyone smiled at this sign of fatherly interest, but when the door had closed behind them he said urgently to Polly, 'The photos? Can I have them now?'

'Of course. I unpacked them ready for you.'

She took the two albums from a drawer and handed them to him.

'Thanks,' he said briefly, and departed without a look at the sleeping child.

* * *

That night Polly stayed up late in her room, telling herself that she was watching over the little boy, but secretly knowing that she was watching over his father. Opening her window and looking out, she could see the glow from his window next door. There was to be no rest for him tonight.

She imagined him turning the pages, seeing 'Sapphire's' face over and over, feeling fresh pain with every new vision.

Why had she let herself be taken by surprise? Deny it how he would, Sapphire had been the woman he'd loved so passionately that a few days ago the briefest imagined glimpse of her had driven him to madness, almost claiming his life. Perhaps he would have preferred that, now *she* was dead. He was, in effect, a widower, but denied a widower's freedom to mourn openly—denied even the memories of a shared love that might have made his loss bearable.

Suddenly she remembered that Freda's wedding pictures were in the second album. In the hurry and agitation it had slipped her mind, but now she wished she'd remembered and removed them. It was too late, but she might have spared him that.

A quick glance showed that Matthew was still sleeping. She went out into the corridor and knocked softly at Ruggiero's door.

'Come in.' The words came softly.

He was sitting on the bed, his hands clasped between his knees, the wedding pictures open beside him.

'I just came to see if you were all right.'

'I'm fine—fine.'

She sat on the bed beside him.

'No, you're not,' she said gently. 'I've been watching you all evening, and you're like a man stretched on a wheel. Your nerves are at breaking point—even your voice sounds different.'

'Different how?'

'Tense. Hard. Every five minutes you ask yourself if you can survive the next five minutes, and then the next. You smile at people and try to say the right things, but it's taking everything out of you.'

'Am I really as transparent as that?' he asked, with a brief wry smile.

'No, I don't think anyone else has noticed.'

'Just Nurse Bossy-Boots, keeping an eagle eye on the patient?'

Or a woman with a man whose every word and gesture means something, she thought, and longed to be able to say it aloud.

He sighed and squeezed her hand. 'No, it's not just your being a nurse. You see things that nobody else does. Where do you get it from?'

She resisted the impulse to squeeze back, and said, 'In a way it *is* part of being a nurse. You watch people so much that you starting noticing odd details. I don't just mean medical things, but about their lives.' She gave a little chuckle.

'What? Tell me.'

'I got so that when a man brought his wife into the ward I could tell at once how things were between them. I knew which husbands were going to be faithful while their wives were in hospital, and which ones were going to live it up.'

'How?'

'Something in the voice. If he called her "darling" every second word I knew he'd be on the phone to a girlfriend before he left the building. The ones who were going to go home and worry didn't say very much, just looked.'

'You've got us all ticketed, then?'

'Absolutely,' she said, trying to ease the mood by making a joke of it. 'No man can spring a surprise on me. You're all boringly predictable.'

There was one man she hadn't told Ruggiero about—a soldier, who'd brought his wife to the ward and had seemed to think he was on parade, talking at the top of his voice and bullying everyone. But afterwards she'd found him sitting in the corridor, staring into space.

'Boringly predictable' had been a joke, and far from her real thoughts. It was that desperate soldier who'd given her the clue to Ruggiero.

He interrupted her thoughts by saying suddenly, 'Does Brian know how you think?'

'Well, I don't talk to him that way. A woman should keep her secrets.'

'From the man she loves?'

'Especially from the man she loves,' she said firmly.

'And he doesn't suspect?'

'Not if I can help it.'

'Keep the poor fool in blissful ignorance, eh? I guess that runs in the family.'

He said the last words so quietly that she didn't need to respond to them, but their bitterness wasn't lost on her.

'What kind of man is Brian?' he asked suddenly. 'Does he tend to be faithful, or go the other way?'

'I've hardly had time to judge.'

'But with you being so preoccupied this last year—you weren't afraid that he'd stray?'

'I haven't been putting his fidelity to the test,' she said, with perfect truth.

'Is that because you're afraid to try, or because he doesn't have enough spirit to be unfaithful?'

'You make infidelity sound like a virtue?' she said, half laughing.

'Not exactly. But to be as sure of him as you are—he sounds like a suet pudding.'

'I promise you he's not a suet pudding. Brian's lively enough, but he spends long, exhausting days looking after people who need him.'

'And when you get together you talk about test tubes. That must be thrilling.'

She hadn't wanted this discussion, but it was useful. Being close to Ruggiero like this affected her so strongly that she was terrified he would sense it, and Brian was a useful shield. So she played along.

'Anything can be thrilling if you share the same interests,' she mused.

'And that's what you talked about when you saw him yesterday?'

She chuckled. 'I don't think we talked much.'

'But didn't he try to persuade you to stay with him—in between doing whatever you were doing?'

'No, of course not.'

'Of course not? Does he love you or not?'

'He does, but he knew I had to come back for as long as I'm needed here. He understands about putting duty first.'

'Another thing you share?'

'Another thing we share.'

'You told him that you're crazy about him but you had to return to this grumpy so-and-so who'll collapse without you? That *and* test tubes? How did you tear yourself away from such passion?'

'Nurse Bossy-Boots never lets down a patient,' she said primly. 'And passion can be found in the oddest places.'

She found she was enjoying this conversation too much for safety, and hurried to say, 'But I don't think I ought to discuss him any more. He wouldn't like it.'

Ruggiero threw her a grim look. His nerves were stretched from the two tense days he'd spent waiting for her, wondering if he would ever see her again.

He was a man with no gift for self-analysis. He could dismantle an engine both actually and in his head. He even had some faint understanding of others. But to himself he was an almost total mystery.

In the last two days he'd been miserable, thinking of the pictures that Polly might or might not remember to bring back. He'd focused on that because he understood it, but somewhere along the line it had blurred with the fear that she might not return at all.

Arguments had raged in his head. His strong, reliable Nurse Bossy-Boots was a woman of her word. She wouldn't let him down because that wasn't her way. But the ties holding her back were immense—including the man she loved, who might be fed up with waiting and demand to come first in her life.

Perhaps she'd give the pictures to Hope and leave, confident that she'd done her duty?

But she wouldn't have done it, he told himself firmly. She was the one person he could talk to, and she had no right to desert him.

Hope had called him that morning to say they were returning together. He'd breathed again, but even so he'd been shocked by the explosion of relief that had attacked him when she'd appeared at Naples Airport. It had the perverse effect of making him abrupt, even angry with her. And this, too, he did not understand.

CHAPTER SIX

His eyes were on the photographs. Sapphire. Briefly she'd faded, but now she flamed back into his consciousness, as sharp and poignant as ever. He drew in a sharp breath at the sight of her radiant beauty on the day she'd married another man.

'They're lovely pictures, aren't they?' Polly said.

She began to turn the pages. Freda had been at her best on that day: her extravagant beauty flaunted in a glamorous satin creation, George's wedding gift of diamonds on her head, holding in place a veil that stretched to the floor.

There she was with her new husband, looking adoringly into his face because she wanted to be convincing in her role. George had been good for several more diamonds yet.

There she was with her chief bridesmaid, poor cousin Polly, looking horribly out of place in a frilly pink satin dress, her dullness cruelly contrasted with the bride's lustrous looks.

One picture was a close-up of Freda alone, with a soft, sweet smile and a tender expression that had seldom been there in real life. She'd been an accomplished actress, and for this shot she'd managed to banish the gleam of greedy triumph from her eyes. The woman in that picture was enchanting: soft, generous, giving, yielding; everything that she had not been.

'I'm sorry,' she murmured. 'I shouldn't have brought the wedding pictures.'

'Why?' he asked sharply. 'Do you think I'm afraid of them?'

'Perhaps you ought to be. What difference can it make now?'

'Don't say that. I can't rid myself of her just because she's dead. In some ways I feel I've only just met her, and I need to know everything.'

She shook her head, but she didn't say aloud what she was thinking—that 'everything' was precisely what he couldn't endure knowing. Instead she begged, 'Let the past be. It's the future that matters—your future and Matthew's.'

'But the future grows out of the past. What do I do if the past is a blank? I need to find out as much as I can, then maybe—I don't know. Maybe things will be different. If I could see the places where she lived, get some picture of her life in my mind—you could take me back there.'

'Ruggiero, no.'

'But you could. We could go to England tomorrow. We don't have to be away for long—just long enough for me to see where she lived and go around the places she knew—'

She seized his good shoulder, giving him a little shake.

'It won't bring her back,' she said fiercely. 'Stop this!'

'I can't,' he said in agony.

Looking at him closely, she saw that he was in the grip of a powerful force that was devouring him. His eyes were full of a terrifying obsession. His hot breath brushing her face might have come from the fires of hell.

'Stop it!' she said. 'Stop it!'

'How?' he asked bleakly. 'Help me, Polly. You're the only friend who can. Nobody else knows—I can't tell anyone—how could I?'

It was true. Hope knew roughly what had happened, but not how deep his pain went. Because he loved his mother he would conceal the worst from her, but it left him with nobody to turn to except Polly.

'All the time you were away,' he went on, 'I kept hoping for a miracle. Somehow I'd get things into perspective and see her clearly—that's what I thought. And when you brought the baby back,

I know I was supposed to take one look at him and
be overcome with fatherly love.'

'No, that's only in sentimental films,' she said.
'I think what really happened is that you looked at
him and thought, Oh, my God!'

'O, mio dio!' he agreed. 'Call me a monster if
you like, but I feel nothing for my son. Nothing.'

'You're not a monster at all. When you look at
him I dare say you don't actually see him, because
there's a brick wall built between you, and you
can't get past it.'

'Except that she's there too—both of her.'

'Both?'

'The beautiful girl who loved me and transformed my life, and the manipulator who took
what she wanted and left me in a desert, without
a backward glance. I don't know which one of
them is real, and until I know more nothing is ever
going to be real.'

'Maybe the reality is a bit of both,' she said,
trying to soften it for him.

'Or maybe I'm simply telling myself pretty fairy
tales—seeing only what I want to see, blocking my
ears to anything that doesn't fit in with my picture:
a weak, foolish man who can't bear to face unpleasant facts?'

'Stop being so hard on yourself,' she said fiercely.
'You haven't recovered from the shock yet.'

'I thought I might find some sort of answer in the child's face, but it seems to change all the time. Sometimes her, sometimes me—'

'And sometimes he's just himself, which is how it should be. That poor little boy, carrying the burden of so many expectations.'

'Do you think I don't know that? They're all looking at him to see if he's a true Rinucci—just as they're watching me to see if I'm feeling the right things. So I do what I have to—kneel down, speak to him—so that they don't think how heartless I am. Nobody must guess the truth except you. Without you to hold onto I think I'd go mad.'

She should be sensible and run away now. She'd already had a warning of the perilous path she was treading. But she didn't want to be sensible. She wanted to take the burden from him, even if it led her further down that path and cost her dear.

Polly put her arms around him, letting her forehead rest against his.

'And you *can* hold onto me. I'll help all I can, but not by creating a dream world for you.'

'I don't want that,' he said softly. 'I want to know what she was like in the real world, and only you can tell me.'

'And will telling you help?' she asked. 'Maybe talking about her will only make it worse?'

His eyes burned with his obsession, warning her of the dangerous direction his mind was taking.

'But it might keep her with me,' he whispered feverishly. 'I'm not ready to let go yet.'

'Even of her ghost?'

'If that's all I can have.'

'Haven't you had enough of ghosts?' she asked passionately. 'She's haunted you for over two years, and she nearly killed you. Don't you realise that?'

'Or you did,' he said wryly.

'No, it wasn't me who sent you spinning off the track into what might have been your grave.'

Something in her brain seemed to snap, and for a moment she went mad, her mind following his down the road to destruction.

'That was her,' she said passionately. 'Because she's jealous and possessive and she can't bear to let you go, even though she doesn't want you. That's how she was. If she couldn't have something, she hated anyone else to have it. Her life was taken, so now she—'

Appalled, she checked herself.

'What am I saying?' she choked. 'I'm talking about her as though—almost as if—'

'That's what she's doing to my head, too,' he told her. '*Now* do you understand that there's no escape?'

'There is if you fight it.'

'And if I don't want to fight it? Do you know

what happened to me that day at the track? When I saw her standing there in front of me I was glad. I knew she was beckoning me to disaster but I didn't care. I was so full of joy at seeing her after so long. I think I called out to her—'

'Yes,' she said, remembering how he'd lain in her arms afterwards and murmured Sapphire's name.

'I was chasing her across a great distance, but she always evaded me, and then she was gone.'

'And you think if I take you back to her old haunts you'll find her? You won't. That's not where the truth lies.'

'But I have to believe that it's somewhere to be found otherwise I'll go mad.'

'Can't it be enough that she was beautiful?' Polly begged. 'That you had a perfect time together and she left you a son?'

'A chimera,' he murmured. 'Nothing more.'

'That little boy wasn't born from a chimera. He's real, and he's all that's left of her. Ruggiero, please, *please* try to understand. *You can't bring her back.*'

He seemed to relax against her, and for a moment she thought she'd got through to him. Moving slowly, she reached out to the wedding album and drew it towards her.

'Let me take this,' she said. 'Don't brood over it.'

But his hand clamped over hers. 'Leave it.'

'Ruggiero—'

'I said leave it.'

Before he could reply she heard the shrill of her cellphone from her room.

'I must answer that before it wakes him up,' she said, and hurried out without closing Ruggiero's door.

From the next room he heard her say,

'I called you earlier today, but there was no answer so I assumed you'd gone to the hospital.'

Then he closed his door, resisting the temptation to eavesdrop further.

In her room, Polly moved well away from the cot and spoke softly into the phone.

'Iris, I'm so glad your daughter's all right. I'm sure she'll be home from the hospital soon. And thank you for everything.'

She hung up and returned to Ruggiero.

'Can I come in again?' she asked through the closed door.

'No,' came his voice. 'I won't disturb you any longer. Goodnight, Polly.'

'Goodnight.'

There was nothing to do but turn away, wondering about the opportunity that had been lost.

The next day Ruggiero announced that he was well enough to go work.

'Is he?' Hope immediately asked Polly.

'Yes, *he* is,' Ruggiero declared firmly.

'Yes, he is,' Polly said, speaking like a robot. Then she laughed and said, 'You heard him. I've been told what to say.'

'The idea of *you* taking orders!' Hope scoffed, giving her an admiring look.

'He'll be all right if he's careful,' Polly said.

'Then we're going shopping,' Hope said gleefully. 'I want to celebrate my new grandson.'

'By stripping the shops bare?' Toni enquired with wry amusement.

'Can you think of a better way of celebrating?'

She, Toni and Polly set off, accompanied by Matteo, as he had now become. Hope was in her element, spending money on toddler clothes, toddler toys, toddler food, turning to Polly for advice and sometimes actually taking it.

'You're not offended with me?' she asked Polly anxiously. 'I know you've always given him the best you could afford—'

'I'm not offended. He was growing out of most of his stuff anyway, and who wants to pass up the chance of a shopping trip?'

Cheered by this sign of Polly's good sense, Hope swept her into a dress shop and bought her the basis of a new wardrobe— 'So that I can be really sure you're not offended.'

'But I'm not—'

'Then accept these few things, with my thanks.'

'Don't argue,' Toni begged. 'Let her have her own way, *please*!'

'All right,' Polly said, understanding him correctly. 'For your sake.'

They all laughed.

The family was gathering, all eager to inspect the newest Rinucci. Later that day Luke and Minnie arrived from Rome, while Primo and Olympia made a second visit. Once more Matteo was in his element, holding court. In a very short time Matteo became Matti.

Ruggiero arrived to find Olympia holding the child up high while they giggled together. He behaved delightfully, kissing his sisters-in-law, joshing his brothers, and later joining in the family amusement at the sight of his father with his grandson on his lap, an adoring slave.

It was a charming scene, but again Polly knew that he was using it as a screen to hide how little he felt for his son. Once she would have blamed him, but now she understood more clearly. Freda's rejection had wounded him as much as her death, perhaps more, and for now the child was merely a reminder of that.

When it was Matti's bedtime Hope came to Polly's room and assisted. When he was in his cot, she leaned down and kissed him.

'Buona notte,' she murmured.

Seeing Ruggiero in the doorway, she beckoned him forward.

'Kiss him goodnight,' she urged.

'Better not disturb him now he's sleeping,' he said. 'I think I'll go to bed now, Mamma. Goodnight.'

Polly spent the next day at the villa with Hope and Toni, enjoying the sight of their rapport with Matti. Hope had noticed that Ruggiero wasn't at ease with the child, but it didn't trouble her greatly.

'It will take a little time for him to relax about this,' she said cheerfully. 'But that's all right. I'm not in a hurry to see him vanish back to his apartment.'

'Apartment?' Polly asked, startled. 'I thought he lived here.'

'He does some of the time, but he has his own place in Naples too. All our sons have homes away from us, but they keep their rooms in the villa.'

'But how will he manage on his own with a child?' Polly wondered.

'He can't. Matti will stay with us at first, and live with Ruggiero later, when he's grown up enough to do things for himself.' She added in an undervoice, 'And when my son has grown up enough to be a father.'

'That's not fair,' Polly said at once. 'It's less

than a week since he knew she was dead, and he's grieving for her.'

'A woman who treated him like that? Polly, have you told him everything yet?'

'No, he's not ready. He has suspicions, but nothing he can't shake off. How can I give him a clear picture of my cousin without also destroying Matti's mother in Ruggiero's eyes?'

They were both silent. Then Hope patted her hand.

'You will find a way. You are a wise woman, and you have all my trust.'

'And mine,' said Toni, who didn't always allow his wife to speak for him.'

The evening meal was early, with Matti sitting on Toni's lap like a little grandee, lording it over his court. There was no sign of Ruggiero, but as they were all climbing the stairs to put Matti to bed the phone rang. Toni went to answer it, and joined them a few minutes later, saying, 'Ruggiero won't be back tonight. After the time he's had off he says he must work late, so he'll go to his apartment.'

He didn't return the next day, or the one after. Polly became more troubled, haunted by the things he'd said to her the night before he'd left, the glimpse she'd had of a tortured mind. She longed to talk to him again—see into his thoughts, help to rid him of his obsession.

Or maybe I just want him to forget her and think of me, she thought with wry realism. Who am I kidding? Not myself, that's for sure. Freda would be the first person to tell me what I'm really hoping for.

And she did.

That night her cousin came to her, dancing out of the misty darkness.

'Freda? What are you doing here?'

The vision laughed, swirling her glorious hair so that it was like a halo. She was in a long, floaty dress that swirled about her, and all her beauty had returned.

'I'm not Freda any more,' she teased. 'Freda's dead.'

'*You're* dead.'

'No, I'm Sapphire now. Because that's how *he* thinks of me, and you've started to see me through his eyes.'

'Go away,' Polly cried.

'You'd like that, wouldn't you? You want to make him forget me so that you can have him for yourself. But you never will. He's still mine. He loves me, and there's nothing you can do about it—nothing—nothing—nothing—'

She was gone.

Suddenly the darkness vanished, dawn light filled the room, and Polly awoke with a shudder to find herself sitting up in bed.

'It was a dream,' she gasped. 'Only a dream.'

She went to the bathroom to splash water on her eyes. The face in the mirror was so superficially like Sapphire's, yet so cruelly different.

'She's dead,' she told the image firmly. 'She's gone for good.'

'But I haven't,' Sapphire whispered in her mind. 'I'm not dead to him. Why do you think he's vanished? He wants to be alone with me.'

Suddenly the fear was hard and real, driving Polly out into the corridor and into Ruggiero's empty room.

A thorough search confirmed her worst suspicions. The photo albums were missing.

The Palazzo Montelio overlooked the Naples docks. Despite its name it wasn't a palace, but a grandiose edifice, built by a self-important merchant who'd wanted a place where he could keep a constant eye on the boats that provided his wealth. For two centuries his fortunes had flourished, but then declined, so that the building had had to be sold and turned into apartments.

As she made her way slowly up the wide stairs to the second floor Polly wondered again if she was wise to come here. But perhaps it had been inevitable since the moment Hope had called Ruggiero's firm and discovered that was not there.

'Not for the last two days,' she said, looking significantly at Polly. She scribbled something on a scrap of paper. 'That's where he lives.'

So now here she was, about to beard the lion in his lair, ready to face his fury at her temerity in hounding him.

But all he said when he opened the door was, 'What took you so long?'

She'd half expected to discover that he'd been drowning his sorrows, but his voice was sober and his movements steady.

The apartment was an odd mixture of faded grandeur and modernity, with old-fashioned comfortable furniture and a gleaming kitchen. She managed to look around cautiously while he made some English tea, which was unexpectedly good.

Now that she could observe him better, her first favourable impression was changing. If he hadn't been drinking, neither had he been eating or shaving. His dark hair meant that several days' stubble stood out starkly, making his lean face almost cadaverous. Nor had he slept much, if his eyes told a true story.

He looked as if he'd dressed in the first thing he'd been able to find to throw on—old jeans, old shirt, mostly unbuttoned so that she could see the rough, curly hair beneath.

'You knew I was coming?' she said.

'I'd have bet money on it.'

'Well, you're still my patient. I needn't ask how you've managed. I can see that you've been taking proper care of yourself, eating well, getting enough rest, behaving sensibly. I can't think why I bothered.'

That made him laugh, and he winced, holding his side.

'It hurts more than it did,' he admitted.

'And it'll go on hurting for a while. I've brought you some more pills. These won't send you to sleep like the last ones.'

'Thanks. I've been trying some that I bought in a shop, but—' He shrugged, then stopped quickly and rubbed his shoulder.

'Here,' she said, producing the pills. 'Take a couple now, and we'll think about something to eat.'

'I don't have much in the place.'

'Then we'll have to go out. My treat.'

'No, I can't let—'

'I didn't ask you to let me. I just said that's what I'm going to do.'

'Yes, ma'am.' He gave a brief snort of laughter. 'You don't know how good it feels to have you bullying me again.' He added abstractedly, 'Maybe my father was right.'

'About what?'

He'd recalled Toni's words about how Hope anticipated his needs and fulfilled them before he was even aware. The outside world might dismiss it as domination, but Toni had spoken like a man with a happy secret. Ruggiero was about to tell Polly, but backed off, realising that this would lead him into unknown paths where perhaps he couldn't rely on her hand to steady him.

What he did know, beyond doubt, was that if she hadn't arrived when she did he would have sought her out.

'Never mind,' he said hastily. 'Poppa says a lot of strange things.'

'Then you're not his son for nothing,' she mused.

She spoke lightly, but the sight of him worried her. How long was it since he'd last eaten? She decided to get some food into him fast.

The light was fading as they left the building. Lamps were coming on in the little restaurants along the seafront, and on the boats that came and went in the harbour.

'They're mostly ferries,' he explained, 'linking us with Capri, Ischia and several other islands.'

'That place looks nice,' she said, pointing at a tiny café near the water. A board over the door announced Pesci Di Napoli.

'Fish from Naples,' she announced triumphantly. 'You see, I've actually learned some Italian words. Let's go.'

'Not there,' he said quickly.

'Why? Is there something wrong with it? Is the fish rancid?'

'Of course not. But there are better places—'

'Ruggiero, mi amico!'

The bawling, friendly voice stopped them as he was about to hurry her away, and made him turn reluctantly.

'Leo,' he said.

The man standing in the doorway of Pesci Di Napoli beamed and shook his hand so vigorously that Ruggiero winced.

'Leo, this is Signorina Hanson, and she only speaks English.'

'Welcome, *signorina*. Ruggiero, it's too long since we saw you. Come in and have something to eat. We've got fresh clams today, and I know how much you like them.'

There was no escape. Ruggiero smiled and ushered Polly in.

'You know this place well?' she asked, looking at him curiously.

'He owns part of it,' Leo said. 'The profits he makes here he throws away on motorbikes, so that he can have the fun of half killing himself. One day he'll complete the job and we'll all have a good laugh.'

Ruggiero grinned at his friend's jeering irony. The atmosphere was warm and jovial.

And yet he'd tried to steer her away.

Leo led them to a table by the window.

'Spaghetti with clams to start with,' Ruggiero said, 'since that's what Leo's decided. And afterwards—'

He explained the menu to her and they decided on *lasagna napolitana* and coffee. Leo tried to interest them in wine, but she shook her head.

'No alcohol,' she said. 'Not with those pills.'

'I know. You told me days ago.'

When Leo had departed Ruggiero asked, 'Did you rush down here to see if I was drinking myself to death? You needn't have. I've stuck to tea, believe it or not.'

'I do believe it,' she said lightly. 'I know that among your many virtues the greatest is self-control.'

'Are you making fun of me?' he demanded suspiciously.

'Why should you think so?'

'My "many virtues"! You wouldn't say that except ironically.'

She was silent, wondering how far it was wise to push him.

'Don't you have many virtues?' she ventured at last.

'Probably not many that you'd call virtues.'

'Perhaps they cease to be virtues when you carry them to extremes?'

'Such as?'

'Self-control is fine, except when you turn it into an iron cage,' she ventured.

'And you think that's what I do?'

'Yes, because you told me yourself. When we first talked about Sapphire you said that what was in here—' she laid a hand over her heart '—was just for you, because it was safer for a man to keep himself to himself.'

He nodded. 'And she lured me out,' he said in a wondering voice. 'That was one reason that I loved her.' He gave a half smile and tried the word again. 'Love. I wouldn't say it because it made losing her so much worse, but with her I talked about things I'd never spoken of before.'

'He never shut up,' said Sapphire grumpily in her head, *'just because I once said, Tell me all about yourself. I mean, it's only a come-on. I always said it to flatter men. But he took it literally.'*

'Then that was something she gave you,' Polly said gently. 'You're better for knowing her. And you'll always have it—unless you slip back to being grim and taciturn.'

'Which I was doing,' he mused. 'Until you took me by the scruff of the neck and yanked me back.'

Averting her head slightly, she made a face. Sapphire enticed. Polly yanked by the scruff of the neck. There it was—the truth about them. But at least it would stop her getting sentimental and foolish.

'Why are you laughing?' he asked.

'Never mind. You wouldn't see the joke. Besides, it's not really funny. Ah, here's Leo with our food.'

She changed the subject, chatting about his parents, and how Matti was ruling the roost, but speaking in a casual way that put no pressure on him.

'He's made himself at home, then?' Ruggiero asked. 'Put his feet up, so to speak, and now he's monarch of all he surveys?'

'That's exactly right—especially with your father. He's Toni's special pet.'

A strange look came over Ruggiero's face.

'Ah, yes,' he murmured. 'At last he's got a grandchild.'

'At last? He already has plenty of them by your brothers, doesn't he?'

'No, they're my mother's grandchildren, not his. Primo was her stepson in her first marriage, Luke was adopted, Justin and Francesco are hers, but not Poppa's. Of course they're all family, and Toni loves them because he has a great heart, but only Carlo and I are his actual sons. Carlo's wife is too frail to risk children, so that just leaves me.'

Suddenly Ruggiero sat back in his chair, transfixed.

'No wonder that little kid has taken Poppa by storm. Why didn't I see it before?'

There were a thousand answers, but the one that warmed Polly's heart was that out of the turmoil of feeling that had invaded Ruggiero in the last few days had come a new and generous understanding of his father.

'I'll give you another reason,' she said, smiling. 'Matti looks like him. We've all been staring into that little face, trying to decide whether he resembles you or his mother, but actually it's Toni.'

'You're right! I should have noticed that.'

'Maybe you need to stand back a bit to see things clearly?' she said, giving the words two meanings.

He nodded. 'Maybe.'

'Eat your food before it gets cold.'

'Yes, Nurse.'

CHAPTER SEVEN

As THEY ate Polly studied him. He might only have been starving for two days but it looked more like a week. What had happened while he'd been shut up alone with those photographs and his pitifully few memories?

And then she knew why he hadn't wanted to come to this place.

Her cousin was there in her mind again, as she'd been in the last few weeks of her life, giving one of her cruel monologues in a voice that had begun to rasp.

'He used to talk about how we'd go to Naples together and he'd take me to this little fish restaurant he part-owned. He said he'd show me off to all his friends—as if I wanted to be displayed to a load of fishermen! No, thank you! He thought he was really something, but he didn't have a clue.'

That was why he hadn't wanted to bring Polly

here. In his mind it was reserved for Sapphire. He'd never known that she'd appreciated him only for his skill in bed. When he'd grown sentimental she'd despised him.

Get out, she told the evil imp in her head. You don't deserve him.

But the imp was clever. She changed, becoming beautiful again.

'And you think you do?' she jeered. *'Do you think you'll take him from me by mothering him? I know what he wants from a woman, and it isn't that.'*

I'll free him from you, no matter what I have to do.

Sapphire vanished, sulking, as she'd always done when she didn't get her own way easily.

'Are you all right?' Ruggiero asked. 'You went strange all of a sudden.'

'Yes, everything fine. This food is good. Tell me, did you ever go into work?'

'Yes, but after the first day I realised I wasn't ready.'

'And you always meant to come back to your apartment. That's why you took the pictures of Sapphire.'

He avoided answering this directly, but gave her a curious look.

'Do you know that you just called her Sapphire?' he asked. 'It was always Freda before.'

'I didn't realise. Well, it's awkward if we're using different names.'

But that wasn't the reason, she knew. Freda had gone. Only Sapphire existed now. Increasingly she had the feeling that her enemy was taking shape before her, ready for a fight that was inevitable.

'I'm not a very good host,' he said with a faint smile. 'When a man takes a woman for dinner he should talk about her—her eyes, her face…'

'You try that and I'll make you sorry,' she threatened, her eyes gleaming.

'Ah, yes. Brian wouldn't like it.'

'*I* wouldn't like it. I'm here to look after you. Your mother hired me as your nurse, and I'm going to earn my salary.'

'My mother's *paying* you?' he asked, in a voice that sounded surprised and not entirely pleased.

'Certainly. I'm providing a service and she's paying the going rate. Well, more than the going rate, if I'm honest, but that only means I have to be more conscientious about doing my job.' A burst of inspiration made her add, 'Brian's very pleased. Getting married is expensive, and we're neither of us earning much yet, so the longer this job goes on the better he likes it.'

'Even though it takes his heart's desire away from him? Why do you make that face?'

'Why do you say such silly things?'

'Aren't you his heart's desire?'

'I'm English. We don't talk like that. Stop trying to make fun of me.'

'I didn't mean to. It's just that you never seem to come at the top of his list of priorities. He's not exactly burning with passion, is he?'

'I have no complaints,' she replied primly.

'But isn't he bothered by the time we spend together? Why isn't he here, threatening me with dire retribution if I dare lay a hand on you?'

Her lips twitched.

'For three reasons,' she said. 'First, I've assured him that you're an invalid who couldn't lay a hand on a rag doll. Second, if you tried I'd knock you into the middle of next week. And third, I'm getting good money to put up with you.'

Ruggiero joined in her laughter.

'Completely unanswerable,' he conceded. 'So I don't have to feel I'm imposing on your kindness if I ask another favour?'

'What favour?'

'Come back with me now, and fill in some more of the blanks.'

'If I can remember,' she hedged.

'I think you can remember everything, and you must tell me whatever I ask. Promise me that?'

Luckily he didn't wait for her answer, but called Leo and rose to leave.

True to her promise, she tried to pay for the meal. But Ruggiero scowled until she gave up, and they left with his arm around her shoulder.

'You don't mind propping me up, Nurse?' he asked lightly.

'Not at all,' she said, matching his tone. 'I shall put it down as overtime.'

Once in the apartment, he took out the albums and laid them on the table between them.

'Have you spent these last days going through these?' Polly asked gently

'Stupid, isn't it? I turned off the radio and television, made no calls, shut out the world in every way I could so that I could be alone with her. But—' He sighed.

'Ruggiero, don't you realise that I could say anything? How will you know what to believe?'

'Because I trust you,' he said simply.

'But how do you know that you can?'

He shook his head. 'I can't tell you that—just that all my instincts say that you're one of the most honest people I've ever met. I trust you as I'd trust my own family. I'd risk my life on your word.'

It was a crushing responsibility, but if she ducked it she couldn't help him, and that was all that mattered. Nor must he guess how she felt about him. Because that would compromise trust and make her useless. Thank goodness for 'Brian', she thought.

'I'll do my best,' she said. 'I probably knew her better than anyone because I lived with her for years. This picture here—' she flipped back to the beginning '—that's my parents, that's Sapphire's parents, and the two little girls are us. It was a sort of joint birthday party. She was seven and I was eight. My mother died two weeks later in a car accident. 'My dad couldn't cope, so they took me in. It was meant to be temporary, but Dad died a couple of years later, so I stayed on.'

'What did he die of?' Ruggiero asked.

'Pneumonia.'

'I thought doctors could cure that?'

'Mostly, yes. But people still die if they're weak enough to start with. He'd been fading away for a while. He never got over losing Mum.'

After a short silence he said, 'Go on.'

'It was a happy sort of life. There was no money, but we were all fond of each other. People used to say that she was the pretty one and I was the brainy one. Well, she wasn't academic, but she was sharp. All the other kids wanted to be her friend, and I was so proud because she chose me.'

Polly gave a reminiscent chuckle.

'It was a while before it dawned on me that she'd hit on the perfect way of getting me to do her homework.'

His grin lightened the sadness in his face and gave her a moment of happiness.

'I was flattered. I became her willing slave. But she gave full value in return. The others in the gang would have left me out of things. Children don't give you any points for being brainy. But she saw that I was included.'

'How old were you there?' he asked, pointing at the two of them in sequined dresses.

'I was sixteen, she was fifteen, and we're dressed alike because it was the school concert and we did a singing act. I remember that while the rest of us were struggling with teenage acne she was already beautiful. Lord, but we all hated her!'

He frowned. 'You mean the other girls bullied her?'

'Don't make me laugh! We didn't *bully* her. We just seethed helplessly in the background. Mostly she didn't notice, but when she did she loved it. It was a kind of tribute. She knew her own power even then.'

'Her power,' he murmured. 'Yes, I remember that.'

'She had only to snap her fingers and fellers would fall at her feet. It was like a spell she cast— over women, too. You couldn't even hate her when she pinched your boyfriends.'

'Plural?'

'Oh, yes. I used to refuse to take them home because they'd take one look at her and collapse. Then I realised that they'd only tagged along with me hoping to get close to her.'

'But you couldn't blame her for that?'

'Of course not. It was natural to her—like breathing. And in a way I enjoyed it too. She was like a queen, and everyone who knew her was in the magic circle.'

He turned the page and stopped at a picture of the two girls and an awkward-looking young man. He had his arm about Polly's shoulder, but his eyes were on Sapphire. Polly was regarding him with almost a glare.

'Who's that?'

'That was my fiancé,' Polly declared with a touch of tartness. 'And this picture must have been taken at the exact moment he started to have doubts. I was madly in love with him—at least I thought I was. She just—I don't know—smiled at him. And suddenly he was hers.'

'She probably didn't even know she was doing it,' he remarked.

Oh, she knew all right, Polly thought. She didn't even want him. He was too poor to really interest her, but she couldn't bear the sight of a man who hadn't fallen under her spell.

But she and Sapphire had declared a truce for

tonight so she only said, 'You're probably right. It hurt a lot at the time, but I don't think she realised.'

'And yet you cared for her when she was ill?'

'I'm a nurse. Looking after people is something you learn to separate from your feelings or opinions.'

'I should have realised that. So what happened to this man? Did you get him back? Is he the one you're engaged to now?'

Polly gave a soft chuckle. 'Heavens, no! Why would I want him after that?'

'You couldn't forgive?'

'It wasn't a question of forgiveness. I just couldn't take him seriously again.'

'You thought, How can I be interested in a man who's shown himself such an idiot?' Ruggiero said lightly.

'Well, I think my so-called "love" was only a juvenile crush, so it died very easily when he fell off his pedestal.'

'How lucky that you found Brian, a man of good sense. How did you meet him, by the way? In the hospital?'

'Yes.'

'Was it love at first sight?'

'No, of course not,' she said sharply.

'Why do you say it like that?'

'I don't believe in love at first sight. It's just a sentimental myth.'

'Maybe it is,' he said thoughtfully. 'Or maybe not.'

He met her eyes, and for a moment the air was full of the things she couldn't say.

Don't you know by now that it's just a myth? If any man should have learned that, it's you.

But the words were too cruel to speak.

And in that moment she knew what she was going to do. If a kind lie was needed to make him happy, then she would tell that lie. It might not be the path of virtue, but that mattered less than nothing beside the need to bring him some inner peace.

'The thing was,' Polly said carefully, 'that she attracted so much love that it was easy to envy her without seeing what she didn't have. She knew something was missing—or at least she'd begun to suspect—and I think inside her she was looking for that something. Maybe she found it with you. I hope so.'

'Did I make her happy?' he asked quickly. 'Did she say so?'

'Yes. She said you were different to the others—kinder.'

What she'd actually said was, *'Honestly, Polly, it was so easy it was boring. I mean, he was a hot-blooded Italian. I thought at least he'd give me a run for my money. But he just collapsed at my feet like the others.'*

'Kinder,' he murmured. 'I'm glad. She needed kindness so much.'

'What makes you say that?'

'On the surface she had everything. But there was a vulnerability about her that I'll swear nobody else had seen, and that drew me to her almost more than her beauty.'

'Men love to think a woman is frail. Just let your voice break a bit, and they fall for it every time. It makes them feel good.'

'But is it kind to delude them?' Polly had asked.

'Kind? Is the world kind? Look at what's happening to me. My looks have gone and I'm dying. Is that kind? You have to use anything that works.'

Kind. Was it that echo that had made her use that word now? It had been chance, but the way he'd seized on it had revealed a new vista.

'You said she might have found what she was looking for with me,' Ruggiero said after a while. 'Did she ever say anything to make you think so?'

'She kept her secrets,' Polly said gently. 'There were things she didn't know how to say. But when she talked about you there was a special note in her voice.'

It had been derision, but he needn't know that.

'Are there any other pictures? From the last year?'

'No, she wouldn't allow that. She wanted to be remembered at her best. This one here is the very last.'

It showed Sapphire holding her child, her cheek resting caressingly against the baby's. The illness had made her thinner, but not yet ravaged her, and she was as beautiful as she had ever been in her life. Ruggiero looked at it for a long time.

'It's late,' Polly said. 'I have to go.'

'Don't go,' he said quickly. 'I have a spare room.' He smiled briefly. 'I'm afraid you might not come back.'

'I'll come back tomorrow if you want me to.'

'No, stay. There's a lot more I want to ask you. And don't worry—you're quite safe. I won't do anything that would bring Brian's wrath down on my head.'

Of course not. Because she wasn't the right woman. She was a lot safer than she wanted to be.

Polly called the villa, spoke to Hope and found, as she'd expected, that Matti was safely in bed.

'Not that it was easy,' Hope complained. 'My husband was playing with him and they were like two babies together. I had to get firm with both of them.'

Polly chuckled. 'All right. I'll leave well alone.'

'You stay there and take care of the other one,' Hope said enigmatically.

'Don't worry. I will.'

Ruggiero showed her the room.

'I've got a shirt if you need something to wear,' he said.

'Thanks, but I have everything I need.' She pointed to her bag.

'But I thought—'

'A good nurse always comes prepared. I could do with some tea.'

'Yes, Nurse.'

She came out a few minutes later to find the tea ready, along with a snack of ham and melon. While they ate she entertained him with tales of the childhood she and Sapphire had shared. It was easier to make her cousin sound sympathetic this way, for in those days her charm had yet to develop its ruthless edge.

Ruggiero laughed at some of the stories and sat contentedly through the rest, sometimes nodding, as if to say that this was what he'd waited to hear.

It was one in the morning before she yawned and said, 'Enough for now.'

'Forgive me for keeping you up so late. And thank you.'

He laid a gentle hand on her arm, nodded, and left her.

Polly put on her pyjamas and got into bed, sitting up and staring into the darkness with her hands clasped around her knees. She had a vague feeling of disappointment that she could not explain.

Sapphire was there in her head—so vivid that Polly could almost see her.

'*Now do you get it?*' she said contemptuously. '*All he wants is the pretty fantasy. Which means he's chosen me.*'

'He needs more time. He'll face the truth later.'

'*How, when you're never going to tell it to him? He doesn't want to hear it. He's not brave enough.*'

'That's true,' Polly agreed sadly.

'*Then I've won.*'

'I guess you have.'

Sapphire gave her luxurious, self-satisfied smile.

'Oh, push off!' Polly said crossly.

Sapphire vanished.

She lay down, listening to the soft sounds of night-time life coming from the harbour until at last she fell asleep.

She was awoken by a hand shaking her gently but urgently. Staring into the gloom, she saw Ruggiero, looking urgently into her face.

'Polly, please wake up.'

She pulled herself up, using him for support, then rubbed her eyes.

'I'll set Brian onto you,' she said through a yawn.

'No need. That's not what I'm here for.'

That was the story of her life. This dangerously attractive man appeared in her room, sitting on her bed, and was she wearing a sexy nightie? No way. She was in austere pyjamas with sensible buttons that came up high. She checked to see if the top button had come undone, but it hadn't. She never had any luck.

'It's all right, you're decent,' he said, seeing the gesture and misunderstanding it. 'Don't worry.'

'I wasn't,' she sighed. 'Ruggiero, what's happened?'

In the darkness she knew that he was glaring.

'Let's say I've finally come to my senses,' he said harshly.

'What—exactly—do you mean?'

'Do you need to ask? Haven't you been waiting for me to let go of the damned fool fantasy and get real?'

He switched on her bedside light and showed her the album that he'd put on the bed before waking her.

'Here,' he said.

The book was open at a large, glossy picture of the bride and groom, standing just outside the church. The photographer had been an expert, and had caught every unappealing detail about the groom—including the fact that he was a good thirty years older than his bride, and at least five stone overweight.

Even that might not have mattered. Many an ugly man had won a woman's heart with love and kindness. But George Ranley's overflowing jowls showed only the greasy self-satisfaction of a man who was selfish, greedy, demanding, suspicious and thoroughly unpleasant.

'Look at her.'

Ruggiero pointed to where the bride was regarding her new husband with a look of adoration. 'Did you ever see so much love in a woman's face?'

'No,' Polly said cautiously.

'For *that thing*?' he asked, pointing contemptuously at George. 'The man's a pig, but she's looking at him like he's a god.'

'Well, it *was* their wedding. A bride is expected to…' Polly's voice faltered.

'It was an act,' he said. 'I wonder what she was really thinking at that moment.'

'Ruggiero—'

'Just as I wonder what she was thinking when she looked at *me* like that,' he finished quietly.

Polly was silent. There was nothing to say. After a while he spoke again, in a voice full of anguish.

'That was the look she wore for me—the look of a woman who's totally besotted with a man. And he believes it while what she's really thinking is that she's got the poor sap just where she wants him.'

Her heart ached. She'd wanted him to see the truth, but now it was happening she couldn't bear the hurt it would cause him.

'I expect he had a lot of money,' Ruggiero mused, almost casually.

'He was a multimillionaire.'

'Those jewels on her head? Real diamonds?'

'Nothing less. George had seized them back from his third wife.'

'Third?'

'Sapphire was the fourth.'

'Go on. Tell me the rest—and don't sugar it.'

'He desperately wanted a son, and none of the other wives had ever got pregnant. He wouldn't admit that there might be a problem with himself, and kept divorcing them as "useless".'

'Sapphire—Freda—didn't want to be divorced, so when he was away for a couple of weeks she went to London to find someone who would give her a child that she could pass off as his.'

'So she went cruising the bars, looking for a suitable candidate?' he said bitterly. 'I just happened to be there. How did I come to pull the short straw?'

'Your colouring is the same as George's used to be before he went bald, so he'd have been easier to convince. And when she discovered that you'd soon be leaving England it was a plus.'

He winced. A long time seemed to pass before he asked, in a low voice, 'She never cared for me at all, did she? Be honest, Polly.'

'I don't think she did.'

'I was just useful,' he said slowly, as though spelling it out would help him understand. 'When I'd served my purpose I was surplus to requirements. All that mystery that seemed so exotic and romantic was just an efficient way to make sure I couldn't spoil things by following her.'

'I'm afraid so.'

Suddenly he began to laugh. A cracked, bitter sound that was on the edge of madness. He lay back on the bed and laughed and laughed until Polly became scared for him.

'What's funny?' she asked, leaning over, taking his shoulders.

'I am,' he choked. 'It's a great joke. I'm the funniest idiot who ever tramped the streets hunting for something that didn't exist.'

He held her in return, looking up into her face.

'When she vanished I searched for her high and low. Once I'd watched her walk away, so I reckoned she was within walking distance, and I went to every nearby hotel. I described her a thousand times, but nobody knew her. I didn't shave or take any care of myself, and by the end of the week I must have looked like a down-and-out. I didn't eat, because to eat I'd have had to stop, and I couldn't bear to. Sometimes I didn't go back to the hotel at night.

'Finally I gave up, got blind, roaring drunk and ended up in a police cell. The next morning they threw me out and told me to stop bothering "decent people". After that I came home. But that wasn't the end of it. In my dreams I went on searching for her, always thinking she'd be around the next corner, but she never was. At last I realised that she wasn't anywhere, and the dreams stopped. The strange thing is that since I've known she was dead they've come back again. Sometimes I'm afraid to sleep in case I find myself chasing around corner after corner, always finding nothing.'

He sat up slowly, still holding onto Polly.

'I guess part of me has known the truth from the first moment, but I wouldn't let myself face it. Now I have, and I should be glad. If this is how it really was, then there's nothing for me to grieve about.'

Nothing except the end of an ideal. Neither voiced the thought, but it was there in the air between them.

'I don't understand,' Polly said at last. 'You've been looking at these pictures for days. Why has this happened now?'

'I don't know. As you say, I could have seen the truth in her face at any time. I guess I just wasn't ready before. I ducked and dived, and clung to what I wanted to believe—anything to avoid the reality.'

'But what do you think the reality is?' she asked carefully.

'That I'm a fool who fell victim to a clever woman because he was too stupid and conceited to see through her. She acted as though I were the one she'd spent her life waiting for. The only lover who could satisfy her, the one man who could make her life worth living. *Of course I believed her.* I was wide open for it. She must have seen me coming for miles.'

His voice was harsh with the scorn and derision he poured on himself. The more he'd believed in his dream, the more contempt and loathing he felt for himself now.

Polly couldn't bear it. She pulled him into her arms and held him tightly. He clasped her back, as though she were his only refuge. It wasn't the embrace of a lover, and he seemed completely unconscious of her lightly clad body, but he buried his face against her and she could feel him trembling.

In a sudden passion of tenderness she began to stroke his head. She knew it wasn't wise, but suddenly wisdom seemed an abomination when set beside his need. If this moment cost her the rest of her life she would pay the price gladly.

Ruggiero didn't draw away, which emboldened her to lay her cheek against his hair while her hands caressed his body, but only tentatively, half longing for him to sense her, half fearing it.

For a moment she grew still, waiting for his reaction, her heart thumping. If he would only reach for her—

But he didn't move. His body against hers was heavy and relaxed, his head lying against her shoulder in an attitude of contentment. She dropped her head, letting her lips lie against his hair.

He did not react, and something inside her seemed to hide away, weeping.

'Don't…' she murmured.

'What do you mean?'

'Don't be so hard on yourself.'

'It's better if I am. I've been easy on myself for too long. Now it's time to see things clearly. *Mio dio!* What a coward I've been!'

'You're not a coward. You just needed time. And you made it. She was holding you trapped. The illusion was turning to poison and it would have destroyed you. Now you're free.'

'Free?' He echoed the word as though trying to understand it. 'Free.'

It had a hollow sound, as though it resonated only bleakly in his heart.

He drew back and looked at her for a moment.

'I needed you,' he said. 'Thank you.'

But you didn't notice I was here, she thought sadly. Not really.

CHAPTER EIGHT

WHEN Ruggiero had gone Polly dozed fitfully, unable to sleep properly. Even Sapphire didn't manage to storm her way in. She tried, but now something was excluding her.

Polly awoke in the morning, wondering if she'd imagined the night before. But her hand could still feel where he'd gripped it in his as he declared his faith in her, and his need. He'd left immediately after that.

Just a handclasp, but it had left her burningly aware of every detail about him. The things she'd been trying not to think of—the strong, hard feel of him, the warmth of his body when it had lain against hers, all the things a good nurse was supposed to ignore—had all come surging back to her.

I'm not going to let this happen, she tried to tell herself. I'm not.

But it had already happened. It was too late to

deceive herself about that. Last night she'd given in to weakness, allowing her tenderness to flare briefly into passion. If he'd responded she would have done all in her power to make him want her, to make love with him.

But he hadn't responded. He hadn't even been aware of the change in her. She tried to be glad about that, but against her will her flesh was reacting to her memories, growing hot, the skin beginning to tingle with need.

But the need wasn't just physical. His heart craved the help that only she could give, and it was her nature to be strong, reaching out to those who were vulnerable. If she'd met Ruggiero at any other time, when his macho mask was securely in place, she might not have seen behind it, and then she would never have been drawn to him.

Now he would always appear to her as she'd seen him first—stunned, troubled, cast adrift by events over which he had no control.

And if Sapphire had really been banished, mightn't there be a vacancy?

Get real! she lectured herself. *This hasn't turned you into a beauty, so don't think it.*

But her inner voice lacked conviction, and she hummed to herself in the shower.

She found Ruggiero in the kitchen.

'Come and have some breakfast,' he called, in a voice that was firm and cheerful.

'Fine, I could do with some,' she said, matching his tone. 'Can I help?'

'No, just sit at that table and I'll serve you.'

He watched as she went to the table and looked out at the bright harbour, already busy in the morning sun. He was watching for any sign of consciousness on her part, but there was nothing in her voice or her demeanour.

It had been his imagination. He'd lain in her arms, amazed at the sense of peaceful joy that had stolen over him, taking the consolation she'd offered.

But how much *had* she offered? Had he only imagined the way her hands caressed him, her kiss against his hair? Recently he'd been so plagued by hallucinations that he dreaded to discover this was only another. He'd held still, waiting for her to do or say something that would tell him what to think.

But she'd only said, 'Don't be so hard on yourself.' Kind words, but those of a friend, not a lover.

He'd pulled himself together, swallowing something that felt strangely like disappointment. Now he had to do it again.

'How are you feeling after that disturbed night?' he asked, sitting opposite her at the table.

'A bit confused.'

'That's my fault. I've been giving you a hard time. But no longer. We got everything sorted out, didn't we?'

'I suppose so.'

She spoke cautiously, and he smiled, assuming a firm, efficient voice.

'Don't worry. I've got things in perspective. I don't know what took me so long.'

A faint uneasiness began to stir in Polly's brain. This clear-sightedness was surely what she'd wanted, and yet—

Misunderstanding her worried look, he said, 'It's all right, Polly. It's all over. She's gone. After all, she never actually existed, did she?'

Irrationally she wanted to say, *She existed in your heart,* but she was lost for words. She should be glad of his recovery. Instead she felt a creeping dismay that made no sense.

'Freda existed. Sapphire didn't,' she agreed.

'She was an invention—a role she'd decided to play. But then the curtain came down, the heroine vanished, and the idiot was left alone on the stage, not realising that the performance was over.'

'Don't call yourself names,' she said firmly.

'You're right, it's boring.'

'That wasn't—'

'Did I try your patience very hard?'

She shook her head. 'You had something beautiful and I was taking it away. I don't blame you for wanting to hold onto it.'

'Except that it wasn't beautiful,' he said with a shrug. 'It was stupid and dishonest, and it made me weak. I won't let *that* happen again.'

The way he emphasised 'that' increased her unease.

'There's nothing wrong with a little weakness if it means needing people,' she said. 'Trying to be self-sufficient all the time just leads to trouble.'

'You said something like that to me the first time we met,' he remembered wryly. 'In fact you've always had a pretty poor opinion of me. And you were right. I finally stood outside and got a good look at myself. *Mio Dio!* What a sight! But no more. I've got a job to do, and with your help I'm going to do it.'

'A job?'

'I have to learn to be a father to my son.'

The words should have made her rejoice, but she was struck by the cool efficiency of his manner—as though he were ticking off tasks on a worksheet. His love, once so sweet to him, had been revealed as a con-trick—to be dismissed along with the side of his nature that was capable of those feelings. Now his relationship with his son was the next assignment on the list.

She shivered.

'I'd better start with some toys, hadn't I?' he said. 'What does he like?'

'Cuddly things. I don't know what Italian shops sell.'

'Fine, we'll go shopping. That means a taxi. What a pity my car's still at the villa.'

'Makes no difference. I wouldn't let you drive it.'

'Wouldn't *let* me—?'

'Nope. And wipe that outraged look off your face, because it's wasted on me. You've fallen into the hands of a real bully now.'

'I think I'd already guessed that. All right, a taxi it is.'

In the city centre they found a large toy shop and explored it from top to bottom. Polly's mood soared. The day was bright, the sun high in the sky, and his manner was engaging. Surely she was worrying about nothing?

'Why are you looking at me?' he asked once. 'Wait—let me guess. It's the first time I haven't been scowling at you.'

'I ignore scowls. It's just the first time I've seen you looking cheerful,' she teased.

He grinned and put an arm around her shoulder, moving carefully for he was still sore.

'Let's spend some money,' he said.

This wasn't what she wanted from him, but it

was a start. And spending money proved to be as enjoyable as she'd always heard it was.

The toys were dazzling. And an array of magnificent teddy bears rose high on the shelves, making Polly sigh with longing.

'They're so beautifully made it seems almost criminal to give them to a child who'll pull them about,' she mourned.

She selected a fluffy bear with golden fur, about a foot high with large, mournful eyes.

Ruggiero plunged into the important business of explaining his needs to an assistant. Polly couldn't follow the words but she gathered he was doing everything methodically, giving precise specifications—just as if he were ordering spare parts for the factory, she thought.

But he was doing his best, and she appreciated that.

When she saw the collection he'd amassed she stared.

'They're for children developing hand-eye coordination,' he explained. 'He can pull this one along behind him, and he also has to fit the shapes into the right holes. With this one he presses buttons with animal pictures, and it makes noises.'

'What kind of noises?'

'Animal noises. Moo and cluck.'

To demonstrate he pressed the cow button and the cow mooed.

'Let me try,' she said, entranced, pressing the chicken button.

A horse neighed.

'That's not right,' she said. 'That should be a chicken.'

Ruggiero experimented and the same thing happened. He tried the horse button, and a duck quacked. An assistant bustled over, looking concerned.

'Houston, we have a problem!' Polly intoned.

Commotion followed. The staff took out toy after toy, pressing buttons to see if they made the right noises—which they didn't. The shop was filled with the sounds of a barnyard. Passers by stopped and stared in.

The manager was called. He too pressed buttons, without receiving the right sounds in return.

'It's a new consignment,' he wailed. 'They must all be faulty.'

'Do you have anything of the same kind?' Polly asked.

Luckily a similar toy had just come in, based on wild animals, which turned out to be properly connected. Lions roared like lions, elephants trumpeted like elephants, baboons gibbered. Everyone was happy, if slightly hysterical.

'We'll take this one,' Ruggiero said with relief. 'And these.' He indicated all the other toys that he'd collected.

'Aren't some of them a bit complicated for a toddler?' Polly asked.

'Maybe not. Maybe he's brighter than we all think.'

'Of course he'd bound to be a genius with such a father,' she said caustically, and he smiled.

He then tried to carry them all out of the shop—which was mistake since neither his ribs nor his shoulder were ready.

'We need to call a taxi from the nearest firm,' she said.

'Nonsense. I'll be all right in a minute. We just have to pick one up outside.'

Polly didn't waste time answering this. Instead she turned to an assistant and tried to request him to telephone for a taxi. After some confusion he understood.

'Why didn't you help?' she asked Ruggiero.

'Because I was having too much fun watching you.' He added provocatively, 'You must allow me a few innocent pleasures.'

'I've just remembered I forgot to bring your pills with me,' she observed casually.

His horrified stare was very satisfying. He wasn't the only one who enjoyed innocent pleasures.

When the taxi drew up at the villa Hope came flying out, eager to see them, but even more eager to tell her news.

'Carlo and Della are here,' she said, bursting with excitement. 'Della was a little tired, so they came home early.'

Polly recognised Carlo from his picture in the paper. He was a big man with gentle manners that charmed her. He shook Polly's hand warmly.

'I've wanted to meet you ever since I heard what you did for this one,' he said, inclining his head to his twin. 'Not that I can see why anyone should bother to save his miserable life—'

'Get lost,' Ruggiero said amiably.

'I didn't save his life,' Polly hastened to disclaim.

'The way I heard it you tore onto the track and bore him off to safety. Anyway, I'm grateful. I've kind of got used to having him around, and he has his uses.'

Ruggiero grinned, evidently accepting this manner of talking as normal. Carlo brought forward his wife, his arm protectively about her. She was an elegant woman, with such a slight build that she almost seemed to vanish against him. It was clear that she was several years older than her husband, and her frailty showed in her face, but her eyes were bright and sparkling with life, and she hugged Polly with delight.

'As soon as I heard about you and Matti I made Carlo bring me home,' she said. 'We don't often have a sensation like this.'

'Careful, *cara*,' Carlo said, still with his arm around her.

'I'm all right—stop fussing,' she chided him in an under-voice, but she smiled as she spoke, and he didn't remove his arm.

It was pleasant to watch this pair of lovers. The bond between them was shining, complete, and Carlo's care of his wife seemed to bring him a quiet joy that Polly found moving. Glancing at Ruggiero, she found that his eyes, too, were fixed on them, and there was a sadness in his face that was at variance with his earlier cheerful demeanour.

Then, as if his mind was wide open to her, she saw that he thought this was how it might have been between himself and Sapphire if she'd reached out to him in her illness. Instead she'd waited until she was dead before letting him know, so that she didn't have to be bothered with him. Put like that it was cruel, brutal. But it was the truth, and her heart ached for what it did to him.

Then he caught her eye, and the grin was swiftly back in place.

'A great couple, my brother and his wife,' he said. 'You'll like them.'

But just as she could read his mind, he could read hers, and he hastened to say, 'It's all right. I told you—it's in the past. Where's my son?'

Toni was there with Matti in his arms, pointing to Ruggiero and saying, 'Poppa.' He came to stand a few inches away from Ruggiero, and stood surveying his son, while his son surveyed his own son cautiously. Matti regarded them both with aplomb.

Finally he delivered his opinion, turning and putting an arm about his grandfather's neck, and closing his eyes.

'Now I know where I stand,' Ruggiero said comically. 'My son is bored by me.'

'Try a toy,' Polly suggested, and nudged Matti with the teddy until he opened his eyes. 'Here.'

She put it into his hands. He dropped it on the floor.

'Careful—it's so lovely,' she said, lifting the bear and offering it again.

He tossed it back onto the floor.

'Let's see if I do any better,' Ruggiero said, turning to the bags that contained the toys.

Toni set Matti down on the floor and watched as one toy after another was displayed to him. He immediately chose the trolley, causing Ruggiero to cast a look of triumph at Polly, and began staggering across the floor with it. At the fourth step he sat down and gave a yell of annoyance, then immediately got to his feet again and staggered forward some more. This time he managed five steps before sitting down, and everyone applauded.

'*Un miracolo,*' Toni said in delight. 'What a child!'

Suddenly there was a glad cry, and someone shouted, 'Look who's here.'

The next moment Luke and Minnie came into the room.

Hope ran towards them, arms outstretched. 'You made it!' she cried.

'It's only a hundred and fifty miles to Rome,' Luke said. 'Nothing to a brilliant driver.'

'So you think you're a brilliant driver?' his mother challenged him.

'No, I meant her,' Luke said, indicating his wife. 'She's a much better driver than I am—as she'd be the first to tell you.'

Next to arrive were Primo and Olympia, eager to join the throng of admirers. Polly gathered her things and prepared to go upstairs, but Hope detained her.

'Now you'll wear some of your new clothes,' she said. 'You haven't worn them since I bought them for you.'

'But that's because they're so fine,' Polly protested. 'And I've been working.'

'Yes, and jeans and sweater were all right for that, but this is different. Now, please go and put on one of the dresses I bought you—the green one, I think.'

Polly hurried upstairs to put on the dress—which, she had to admit, suited her. Hope had an unerring eye for colour and fashion, and the green silk was quietly elegant in a way that suited Polly's gentle looks.

She was glad of it when she returned downstairs and saw that she could hold her own with the prosperous, well-dressed Rinuccis. Even so, she was glad to stay in the background, simply keeping a careful eye on Matti, who was centre-stage, charming everyone, especially Carlo and Della, who hadn't met him before.

A pleasant feeling was beginning to steal over her. This was a family as she had always dreamed of families. With such people there could be no loneliness such as there was in her own life. Matti would be safe and happy with them.

At last they all sat down to eat supper at the big table, and she felt the magic circle enclosing her too. Ruggiero caught her eye across the table, grinned, and embarked on the story of the toyshop. She joined in, making animal noises where necessary, to everyone's delight. In the exchange of witticisms that followed Ruggiero reminded her that she'd once threatened to knock him into the middle of next week.

At this the whole family roared their laughing approval, and Polly was sure she heard some applause. Hope even grasped her hand, saying, 'That settles it. You must marry him and keep him in order.'

Perhaps Polly had drunk a little more wine than usual, or she might not have dared to laugh and say, in a teasing voice, 'I'm not sure I want a man I have to keep in order. It might be boring.'

'Or it might not,' Ruggiero murmured over the rim of his glass. 'Think of the fights we'd have.'

'Non-stop,' she agreed. 'You risking your neck with some tomfool nonsense, me trying to prevent you, you growling, "Stop making a fuss, woman."'

'Then you hitting me over the head—'

'You make it sound irresistible.'

Everyone laughed again, and the joke was allowed to die. But something had changed. Whether by chance or design Hope had mentioned marriage between them, and that word would lodge in everyone's brain. As, perhaps, she had meant it to.

After supper Polly glanced at the clock. It was Matti's bedtime, but nobody wanted to let him go and she relented.

He was giving a performance—going through his new toys, dealing with the 'difficult' ones with a skill that had Ruggiero grinning as triumphantly as though he'd achieved a personal success—as, in a sense, he had.

Matti was at ease with the shapes, pushing one then another into the right holes to loud applause. Ruggiero was looking pleased with himself, and with his son.

He's cracked it, Polly thought. It was going to be so difficult, but then suddenly he found the way to get on Matti's wavelength. Or Matti found the way. Make his father proud of him, that's the secret, and he got there at once. The others all adore him. He really doesn't need me now, and soon it'll be time for me to go.

She felt a pang of dismay, and not only at the thought of leaving Ruggiero. She loved Matti too, but now he was dismissing her as no longer needed. Perhaps he'd inherited that iron-willed trait from his mother? she thought sadly.

In this mood, she was totally unprepared for what happened next.

Matti was playing with the trolley, pushing it back and forth until suddenly it went over onto its side. He made a grab at it, tried to haul it upright, and failed. A little choke of distress burst from him.

'Never mind,' Ruggiero said. 'I'll do it.'

But Matti didn't seem to hear him. It was as though the tectonic plates of his world had shifted. A minor hiccup that he'd laughed off hours earlier was now a major disaster. His choke turned into a wail, growing louder and louder until it became a scream that went on and on in pitiful agony.

'He's over-tired,' Polly said. 'He doesn't normally stay up this late.'

She had to raise her voice to be heard above the child.

'Shall I try putting him to bed?' Ruggiero asked.

But when he reached out Matti fended him off.

'Mummy!' he screamed. *'Mummy!'*

'It's you he wants,' Ruggiero said.

'No, not me,' Polly said sadly. 'I'm not his mother. Freda was, and she's the one he's crying for.'

She dropped down to one knee, trying to take Matti in her arms, but he lashed out, arms flailing in all directions, until one of them caught her a stinging slap across the face, which made him howl louder.

'Mummy—Mummy—MUMMEEEE—'

'Doesn't it help that he knows you?' Ruggiero asked desperately. 'He must be close to you, too.'

'Yes, but he wants his mother, nobody else.'

By now Matti had lain down on the floor, pounding the hard tiles and shrieking, *'Mummy! Mu-mmy! MUMMEEEE—'*

Polly raised him, going to the sofa and sitting down with him on her lap. She was ready to dodge another blow, but there was none this time, and the little boy simply collapsed against her, sobbing in helpless despair.

Polly rocked back and forth, shattered by the suddenness of his collapse, and frightened by what she felt happening deep inside herself. The child's grief seemed to reach into her, awakening her own, tearing her apart. At last something broke in her, and she too began to weep. She tried to keep control, but the tears streamed down her face, mingling with Matti's tears.

'I'm sorry, darling,' she choked. 'I'm so sorry. I know I'm not the one you want. I know—I know—'

'Mummy,' he wailed softly, his face buried against her.

'I wish I could have kept her alive for you—I did all I could—I did try—but I couldn't—I couldn't—'

She gave up and dropped her head, so that her cheek rested against his hair while anguish welled up inside her and overflowed. At this moment she no longer remembered the self-centred predator who'd used her beauty without scruple. She saw Freda as she'd been in the last months her beauty gone, her life slipping away, her eyes filled with fear—and she was consumed by love and pity.

The family exchanged appalled looks, and the women began to move closer to where they could reach out and offer comfort. But Ruggiero stopped them with a gesture, and it was he who went to

Polly and dropped down on one knee beside her, resting a hand on her arm. He didn't speak, but he stayed like that while she tried vainly to control the violence of her feelings.

'Polly,' he said gently. 'Look at me.'

She shook her head. She didn't want anyone to see her face.

'All right,' he said. 'But let's take him to bed.'

She nodded, unable to speak.

'Come on,' he said, urging her to her feet.

The others stood back as she rose with Matti in her arms and left the room, guided by Ruggiero. Hope gave him a nod of approval as he passed.

When they reached her room he opened the door, standing back while she carried the child in.

'I'm all right,' she choked, sitting down on the bed.

He took a paper handkerchief from a box and used it to dab her face. She pulled herself together by force.

'You're still crying,' he said.

'No, I'm not,' she gasped, through a new bout of sobs.

He didn't answer, but sat beside her, his arms about the woman and child, listening to their mingled weeping, saying nothing, waiting until they were ready, however long it might take.

CHAPTER NINE

AT LAST Polly's shoulders stopped shaking and she managed to grow calmer.

'I'm all right now,' she said.

He didn't believe for a moment that she was all right. She was pretending because she refused to think of herself. He wondered just how often she did think of herself.

But all he said was, 'Let's put him to bed.'

She looked down at where Matti lay in her arms, calmer, but still weeping quietly, and kissed him.

'Come along, darling.'

'Where do you keep his night things?' Ruggiero asked.

'In that drawer.'

He drew out some clothes and watched while she undressed Matti and changed him.

'Why don't you help me put on his night suit?' she said.

But he shook his head.

'He doesn't want a stranger right now. You're all he has to cling to.'

He pulled back the covers for her as she laid Matti into the cot. He was asleep almost at once.

'And now he's as good as gold,' Ruggiero mused, looking down at him.

'He's always as good as gold,' Polly said quickly. 'That wasn't a tantrum. He was confused and miserable because he's missing his mother, and he screamed at the world because that's all a toddler knows how to do.'

'Not just a toddler,' Ruggiero said. 'Isn't that what I've been doing—screaming at the world? Only I don't have his excuse. I told you, I don't like the sight of myself right now.'

He touched the tiny hand lying outside the cover.

'Maybe he and I can help each other,' he murmured. 'We seem to speak the same language after all.'

'I should have seen it coming,' Polly said regretfully. 'So much has happened to the poor little mite—'

'But what about you?' he asked, looking at her.

'I'm all right,' she repeated, but already the tears were sliding down her cheeks again. 'I don't know why—just—suddenly—'

'It was bound to happen. You've had to be strong for a long time, but nobody can be strong for ever.'

'I'm a nurse. Being strong is—is—what I do.'

'Even a nurse is human.'

'I'm used to looking after sick people,' she whispered. 'But when it's someone of your own, for months—I did want to help her—but it was beyond anything I could do. I watched, and tried to make it a little easier for her, but I never did any real good. I couldn't—I couldn't—'

It was happening again. As one wave retreated another engulfed her. She began to pace up and down, weeping, not looking where she was going until she found herself facing the wall and laid her head against it, unable to do anything else.

He was behind her at once, taking gentle hold of her, turning her to face him and putting his arms about her.

'Let it go,' he said. 'Don't fight it.'

She made a vague gesture, almost as if to draw back, but he tightened his arms and then it seemed natural to let her head fall on his shoulder and give way to the grief she'd barely known that she felt.

She felt him drawing her towards the bed, sitting her down and sitting beside her. She seemed to have no energy left, and no hope—nothing but the misery that had consumed her without warning. She sobbed violently, no longer trying to master it.

Polly sensed that he'd turned his head to lay his

cheek against her hair. But he made no other movement until the storm had quietened.

'I want you to tell me everything,' he said gently.

'But I already have. We've talked so much about her.'

'No, we've talked about me,' he said heavily. 'And Sapphire—what she was like, what she did to me. But you haven't told me what it was like for you.'

'That doesn't matter,' she said wildly.

'Do you really believe that? That your suffering doesn't matter? That *you* don't matter? Because that's not how I see it. You've got to tell someone or go crazy—and who should you tell but me, Polly?'

She made an incoherent noise.

'It works both ways,' he urged. 'We each know something nobody else knows, and that can't be brushed aside. Don't hide things any more. Tell me what happened at the end. How did it all come about? How did you find the strength to cope? And don't try to put me off by saying you're a nurse, because that's an excuse, not an answer.'

His insight surprised her.

But something held her silent. This was new territory. To be approached with caution, even a little fear. But his eyes were kind, as though he understood everything that was going through her mind.

'Go on,' he said.

Polly took a shaky breath.

'She was living in Yorkshire, in what George grandly called Ranley Manor, while I lived in south London, near the hospital where I worked. One evening she turned up at my door, holding Matti. George had thrown her out and I was the only close relative she had. That night she only told me that Matti wasn't George's child. The rest came later. At first we were quite happy. She was a good cook, and I ate better than I'd done for ages. Then she told me that she was "a little worried" about a symptom. I knew the truth straight away. I rushed her to the doctor but she'd already delayed too long. We explained that she needed treatment, but not how bad things were. She couldn't have borne to know the worst just then.

'The hospital did everything possible, but it was too late. She wouldn't give up hope. She'd say, "I'm getting better, Pol. I really am." The hardest thing—' She stopped, because the memory that was coming towards her was horrible. She couldn't face it. She could only flee in dread.

'What was the hardest thing?'

'No, it—it doesn't matter.'

'Yes, it does,' he said softly. 'Tell me.'

'Please don't ask me to,' she wept.

'Polly, you've got to deal with it, or it'll fester inside and poison you.'

'I can't—'

'Yes, you can—while I'm keeping you safe.'

He bent his head and kissed her tumbled hair.

'Tell me,' he said. 'Tell me now.'

'She trusted me so much because I was a nurse. She'd say, "I'm all right with you, aren't I, Pol? You're a nurse, you won't let me die." She'd make me keep saying it, because if I said it she knew it was true. *I didn't know what to do*—'

'But you said it, didn't you?' he said sombrely. 'You said what she wanted to hear.'

'I had to,' she said passionately. 'I didn't care if it was true as long as it gave her a little peace, and I lied and lied and lied.'

'Of course. You couldn't have done anything else. Did she believe you?'

'For a while. But in the end she knew, and I could see the fear growing in her eyes. At night she used to sob in my arms. By day she'd put on her bright smile and play with Matti. She was a good mother to him. She liked nothing better than to be with him, playing with him, and when she was too weak to play talking to him. That's why he started talking so soon.'

She drew back a little.

'I've told you the worst of her, but you should know the best too. She was a brilliant mother, and he'll always have that—the knowledge that his mother liked his company best in all the world. That's why her death is so terrible for him. He knows he's lost the loveliest thing he ever had.' She added, almost pleading, 'You should understand that feeling because you feel it too.'

'Not any longer.'

'But for him it's true, and it always will be.'

'What happened at the end?' he asked, not answering her directly.

'She had to go into hospital for the last three weeks. I'd take Matti in, and we'd spend as much time together as we could. When she died I took her back to Yorkshire, to be buried with her parents.'

'And then you came here?'

'Not at first. Matti and I went home, locked the door and stayed there for a couple of weeks. During that time I read the letter that gave me a rough idea where to find you.' A shudder went through her. 'I thought I had everything under control, and then suddenly—'

'It hit you out of the blue,' he said softly. 'When that happens it's terrifying, especially if you're a person who likes to be in control.'

'I guess you could say that about both of us,' she murmured.

'Yes, and it's worse for us because we've got no practice in being helpless,' he said with a touch of grim humour, adding, 'Although I may be learning.'

She gave a choke of laughter

'That's better,' he said, holding her face between his hands. 'No, you're not really laughing, are you? You've borne too much alone, but you're not alone now. I'm here, and I understand you as nobody else does—just as you understand me as nobody else does or ever will. We're a great team.'

She tried to smile, but it came out wonky. The sight touched him painfully, and he drew her closer, kissing her cheeks, her eyes, her lips, thinking of nothing except consoling her.

Polly remained still in his hands, feeling the light touch of his lips with the force of a thunderclap.

'Out of the blue,' he'd said. 'Terrifying—'

His words had been strangely prophetic. There'd been no warning of this, no time to steel herself against temptation and the shock of desire. She could only sit there, helpless in his hands, a prey to the sweetest feelings she had ever known, while he kissed her as if oblivious to what he was doing.

She wasn't sure whether he tilted her face further towards him or whether she raised it herself, but his lips found hers and lay against them. For a moment her breath seemed to stop. There was something almost terrifying about being given something she wanted so much—like being transported to heaven without warning.

He kissed her again and again, while her heart pounded and she tried to think. But thinking was impossible. She wanted to move against him, to fit her head against his shoulder and let her lips caress his. Above all she wanted to entice him to explore her, as she longed to explore him.

Then perhaps they could lie back in each other's arms, neither quite knowing who'd made the first move, side by side, inciting each other to pleasure.

She wanted everything. Not just the love of his body but the love of his heart. And that she couldn't have. He'd offered friendship, but that was all. He was way out of reach and she would be foolish to read anything into this sweet moment. But it was hard when she wanted him so badly, and she could feel herself weakening. In another moment she would hurl caution to the winds and tell him she was his.

And then she would die of shame.

That thought gave her the strength to press her hand against him, making him raise his head and study her face, frowning.

'I'm fine now—honestly,' she said.

'You don't look fine,' he said gently. 'You look as if you're collapsing inside.'

She couldn't answer, only gave him a shaky smile. She tried to speak, to say wise and virtuous words about being sensible and stopping now. But they wouldn't come, and he drew her close again.

This time it was different. As his mouth touched hers again she knew she had no more strength. She could never make herself put a distance between them because she could never make herself want to.

There was a grunt from the cot.

She felt the breath go out of him. He tensed and looked up. The little cry came again.

The moment was over. She rose and went to Matti, not lifting him but leaning over and stroking his cheek until he quietened down.

Ruggiero watched them for a moment, then slipped quietly out of the room without speaking.

Polly awoke to find herself alone and the crib empty. Looking out of the window, she saw Hope and Minnie down in the garden, taking it in turns to spoon breakfast into Matti's mouth.

She was glad of the chance to think. Last night ideas and sensations had chased themselves around her brain in an endless circle that started and finished in the same place—with the feel of his lips on hers.

Out of it all only one thing was clear. Twice she'd come to the edge of betraying herself, and now she must recover lost ground. The chaos inside her must remain her secret.

By the time she went down for breakfast she had

her mask securely in place. But it was needless. There was no sign of him.

'There you are,' Hope called, coming in from the garden. She was followed by Minnie, carrying the child.

'I crept in to take him so that you could sleep longer,' she said.

'Yes, I saw you out of the window.'

They settled on the terrace with coffee and rolls. Matti was completely recovered, shouting cheerfully at the top of his voice.

'Are you all right?' Hope wanted to know.

'Yes, I'm sorry for all the commotion.'

'Don't apologise. I just hope Ruggiero looked after you properly.'

'Oh, yes, he did.' After a moment she'd recovered her composure enough to say, 'Is he around?'

'He left for work. He'll be back tonight for supper.'

Glad to get away from her, she thought. It would be embarrassing for them to see each other too soon.

Toni appeared and greeted them. Matti waved his arms and made a sound that might, with a little imagination, be understood as, *'buongiorno'*.

'He's becoming bilingual already,' Toni said in delight.

'When I've gone he'll forget all his English,' Polly said.

'Not in this house,' declared Hope, patting her

hand. 'That I would never allow. But you're not going for a long time yet. Don't tell me Brian is causing trouble? Let me talk to him and explain.'

'Oh, no—he's fine about everything.'

'Good, then it's settled. You'll stay a while yet.'

It had a pleasant sound. If only she could be sure that Ruggiero hadn't left early to avoid her.

The suspicion increased that evening, when he was late, arriving halfway through the meal and including her in a general greeting. Afterwards he spent most of his time talking to Luke and Minnie, which was only courteous as they were leaving next day, but Polly couldn't help feeling that there was another reason.

She wondered if she was getting paranoid. It might have been only her fancy that when their eyes happened to meet he looked away quickly. Or it might not.

When it was Matti's bedtime everyone came upstairs. Hope bathed him, but then Toni, who'd been watching with a gentle smile on his face, stepped forward.

'He wants his *nonno* to put him to bed,' he said, speaking English but using the Italian word for grandfather. 'That's right, isn't it?' he asked the tot. 'Because Nonno's your favourite.' In a confiding voice he added to Polly, 'He told me that. Mind you, I think he tells everyone the same.'

'I think he does,' she agreed, laughing.

With practised hands he fitted Matti's nappy onto him, eased him into his night suit and laid him gently into the cot. Hope and Ruggiero were standing just inside the room, watching and enjoying the sight of Toni, completely happy.

'Buona notte, piccino,' he said. *'Buona notte .'*

Everyone waited hopefully.

'Say it,' Toni pleaded. 'You managed *buongiorno* this morning.'

Matti merely gurgled.

'Goodnight, my little one,' Toni chuckled.

From his pocket he produced a small furry toy, which he tucked into the bed under Matti's hand.

'He used to say hallo,' Polly observed, smiling. 'It was the first word he managed. Now he says *ciao*!"

'He learns very quickly,' Hope said.

'Of course,' Ruggiero said in mock offence. 'He's my son. What else would you expect?'

He followed his father forward to kiss the child, looked at him for a moment, then left.

Minnie announced that she was going to bed, ready for an early start in the morning. There was a round of 'goodnights' and Ruggiero drifted away with the other men.

At last only Hope was left alone in the room with Polly. She was peering at the little toy that Toni had left there.

'Toni's really happy, isn't he?' Polly observed. 'I don't know when I've seen a man who doted so much on a child.'

Hope nodded. 'And his happiness makes me happy too,' she said. 'Little Matti has a special meaning for him.'

'Yes, Ruggiero told me that only he and Carlo are Toni's sons, and that Carlo is unlikely to have children because of his wife's health.'

'There's time for Ruggiero to have others,' Polly said.

'But will he? What does he tell you? Can he fall in love again?'

'Maybe. Or perhaps he'll have to find another kind of love—more contented but less glorious. And that could be hard. How could you be sure that—? How would you know that the time had come to give up hoping, and try to live without hi—the other person?'

'It's possible,' Hope said, watching her. 'If there has to be a parting, it helps if you know you're doing what is best for him. But be quite certain that all hope is lost. Don't give up without a fight. Now, *cara*, I must go to bed.' She kissed Polly's cheek. 'Don't stay up late.'

Ruggiero was late home again the next evening, and would have missed Matti's bedtime if Polly hadn't unaccountably forgotten all about it. It was Toni who remembered, and asked if they shouldn't be moving.

'There's no rush,' Polly said. 'He seems to be sleeping happily in your arms, so he won't lose anything if he stays up until his father comes home.'

Toni and Hope's eyes met, and a glance of understanding passed between them.

'You're a wise woman,' Hope said.

She didn't expand on this, but the warm approval in her voice was enough to remind Polly of the marriage joke from before, and she become self-conscious. It was clear that the Rinucci family was mounting a take-over bid for her—which would have been delightful if Ruggiero himself had wanted the same. But she was in confusion about what he wanted from her, and even what she wanted from him.

Could she marry him and live as second-best while another woman still held first place? She had a feeling that the question was growing dangerously near.

At last she heard his car arrive and went out to meet him.

'Matti was just complaining that you weren't here to put him to bed,' she called.

'Really? With the rest of you dancing attendance he actually noticed that I was missing?' he asked lightly.

Reinforcements appeared in the shape of Hope, with Toni and Matti behind her.

'At last,' Hope said.

'I've been away from work too long, and I have vital stuff to catch up with,' he said, a tad defensively.

'You have vital work here, with your son,' his mother said firmly. 'Get on with it and stop shilly-shallying.'

'Yes, Mamma. No, Mamma.'

'And don't be cheeky.' She bustled inside before he could answer.

'Will you please tell Mamma that I'm thirty-one, and grown-up now?' Ruggiero demanded wrathfully of his father.

'When you grow up, I'll tell her,' Toni promised. 'Now, take care of your son.'

Polly stayed back while Ruggiero put Matti to bed, watching but not interfering. He did everything properly now, including giving the child a final hug, tucking him up and kissing his cheek.

But she knew that something still hadn't fallen into place. He was like an actor who'd learned the lines and played the role perfectly, but his heart was missing.

She'd expected him to avoid the subject, but

when he joined her in the garden later that night he surprised her by going straight to it.

'I'm still making a mess of it,' he said, coming to sit beside her on the porch step and sounding frustrated. 'Why? Tell me.'

'You're being too businesslike,' she said gently. 'And he knows. You can't fool him.'

'There must be a way to get it right.'

'There isn't one right way. There's a dozen. And you can't find them. You have to let them find you. It'll creep up on you, and then suddenly you'll realise that this is what works for you and him.'

He made a wry face, full of self-condemnation.

'That sounds easy, but it just doesn't happen.'

'You're trying too hard—watching yourself all the time to see if you've got it right, watching him to see if he's reacting as you want. Stop ticking boxes and let him show you the way.'

'I was hoping *you'd* show me the way.'

She shook her head. 'He's a much better guide than I am. He's such a warm-hearted little thing. He'll love you if you let him.'

'Maybe that's my problem. I'm no good with love—of any kind. I get confused. Why don't you give up on me? I'm a lost cause.'

'*Basta!*' she said, aiming a mock punch at his good shoulder. 'Enough, all right?'

'We'll make an Italian of you yet.'

'Yeah, sure. *Basta* is my one Italian word, and that's only because Matti has latched onto it. You should try saying it to him. He won't take any notice, any more than you would, but you'll be on each other's wavelength in no time.'

'I'll make a note.'

'Don't make a note,' she said, tearing her hair. 'He's not an item on your works schedule.' She took a deep breath, conscious of him giving her a quizzical look that was unsettling. 'I'll make things go right for you two or die in the attempt.'

He gave a laugh. 'Don't do that. How would I manage without you?'

'You're going to have to one day.'

'Yes, I am, aren't I?' he said, sounding almost as though he'd just discovered it. 'It just seems so natural, you being here—'

Ruggiero shook his head, puzzled at himself.

'I've never relied on anyone before. When I was a little kid, just learning to walk, holding onto an adult, I used to snatch my hand away at the first chance because I had to do it alone. Of course I fell flat more often than not. Carlo was the clever one. He'd hold on until he was quite sure. But I had to kick the world in the teeth to show I didn't need anyone's help.'

'Even then?' she murmured, teasing.

'Even then. But with you it's always felt right. The day we met I was clinging to you for safety, even though I didn't know it.'

'In between pushing me away,' she agreed, smiling.

He grinned. 'I sent you flying with a great clout, didn't I?'

'Yes, I seem to remember you did!'

'And the other night Matti did the same thing. Like father, like son.'

'Not exactly,' she chuckled. 'He got the other side.'

He began to laugh, leaning back against the porch, watching her.

'Why do you put up with us?' he asked.

'I can't think. It must be something to do with that generous salary you're paying me.'

'Yes, that must be it.'

A contented silence fell. Leaning back against the other side of the steps, she met his eyes. Was he remembering the last time they had been alone together—what had happened—what had *nearly* happened?

'By the way,' Polly said, as casually as she could contrive, 'I'm sorry I had that screaming fit. I never meant to weep and wail all over you. I don't often do things like that.'

'Not often enough. You released something

that's been building up for the past year, and which needed to be released. I'm glad I was the one there.'

He caught sight of her disbelieving face and said, 'I mean it. I like to pay my debts.'

'You do that in hard cash,' she reminded him. 'And plenty of it. I'm not complaining.'

'Oh, yes, I can't tell you what a good feeling it gives me to know that I'm contributing to Brian's future comfort. I hope you're spending something on yourself?'

'Nope.'

'None of it?'

'What for? I have all I need.'

'Not a pretty dress or a new pair of shoes?' he asked, scandalised.

'Your mother bought me all those new clothes.'

'A luxurious meal out?'

'Sure, with me fighting my way though an Italian menu and reducing everyone to fits of laughter.'

'You're right—it's a terrible prospect. I shall appoint myself your translator for an evening. I know the perfect place. It's time we had an evening out.'

'I don't think so,' she said, remembering her resolve to be sensible.

'I'm your patient and your employer. I have first call on your time. No argument.'

When she didn't reply he asked, 'Are you angry with me?'

'Why should I be?'

'The night before last I came to the verge of—well, forgetting my manners. All right, a little more than the verge. But for a moment you seemed to need me, and I was glad. I felt close to you. Surely you understand that?'

'Yes, I do, but—'

'But Brian wouldn't, eh? All right, I should have respected that. But you can't seriously be afraid of me.' His voice became teasing. 'I've never seen a woman more capable of punching a man's lights out.'

'Not with your injuries,' she said lightly. 'It would be unprofessional.'

'If I offend you I give you leave to forget my injuries and make me sorry I was born.'

'Who is offended?' came a voice from behind them.

'Nobody, Mamma. Polly and I were just planning a night out tomorrow. It's time she had some fun.'

'Of course. What a splendid idea!'

'You see—it's settled,' Ruggiero told Polly. 'We'll do it tomorrow night, before you can change your mind.'

'I didn't know I'd made up my mind.'

'Mamma made it up for you,' Ruggiero said wickedly. 'She's good at that.'

'She's not the only one,' Polly said wryly. But inside her she was smiling. She would have the rest of her life to be strong.

CHAPTER TEN

'ARE we going back to that fish restaurant of yours?' Polly asked as they drove down the hill on the following evening.

'No, this is somewhere different. In the old city. You haven't had time to see any of Naples.'

The phrase 'the old city' meant nothing to her, but she soon found out that it was a place of little winding streets with cobblestones. In this part of town there were no pavements, so that traffic and pedestrians fenced with each other in both directions at once.

Polly loved it at first sight. It was dazzling, colourful and vivid, the narrow streets blazing with light even as darkness fell, because the little shops and restaurants stayed open very late.

'This part of Naples is like a world apart,' he told her.

'I like it better than the conventional world,' she said.

'So do I. People seem more at ease here. Let's have some coffee.'

They dived into a tiny coffee bar, where the owner hailed him as a friend and seated them at window table.

'If I'd known we were coming here I'd have worn something more restrained,' Polly said. She was wearing the elegant green gown given to her by Hope. 'I feel overdressed.'

'Don't worry—you'll be fine in the place we're going,' he assured her.

'That's a relief. I never did master the trick of getting these things right. I was always too dull or too bright for the occasion.'

'Why must you always criticise yourself?'

'It comes from having lived a life full of comparisons.'

'Comparisons with her?'

'Yes, I just got used to thinking of myself as the plain one in the pack.' She chuckled suddenly.

'What?'

'I was remembering a lad who said he was madly in love with me and he wanted to shower me with flowers. I thought that was so charming— until they turned out to be buttercups he'd picked in the park. Poor fellow. I was very hard on him, but I wanted roses. Someone had given Sapphire roses the day before, and she was actually offended because they were the wrong kind. I thought that was so cool.'

'The wrong kind?' he asked, askance.

'They were tea roses. He was a bit of an academic, and he explained that flowers had their own meanings, and tea roses were a way of saying that he would always remember her.'

'Tea roses for remembrance?' he echoed, beginning to laugh. 'I thought that was red roses?'

'No, red roses are for passionate love lasting to eternity,' she said in a reciting voice. 'Tea roses are for peaceful remembrance.'

'I've never heard that before.'

'Neither had she, and when he produced a learned tome to prove it I thought she was going to explode. He only lasted one day, but I was so envious. Roses were romantic. Buttercups were prosaic.'

'I don't think so,' he said unexpectedly. 'How can such rich gold be prosaic?'

'But they're so common,' she objected, surprised and charmed by this hint of a poetic streak. 'You can pick buttercups anywhere.'

His next answer startled her even more.

'Is that what makes things beautiful? Rarity? Does something stop being lovely because there are plenty? You're rather like a buttercup yourself.'

'You mean commonplace?'

'I mean made of gold.'

For once she was lost for words. He was looking at her with a question in his eyes.

'I wish I could see into your thoughts at this minute,' he said softly.

'There's never any secret about my thoughts,' she said, trying not to be aware of her heart thumping.

'You know that's not true,' he said, still watching her but speaking quietly, like a man trying to lure a wild bird to come to him without frightening it.

'It's a pretence,' he went on when she didn't reply. 'You accused me of playing the role of father, saying the right words for the wrong reasons. But you're doing the same thing—playing the role of sensible nurse, steady and reliable, with no inner life of her own.'

'Which is how I'm supposed to be—'

'But now I know better. Don't forget that. You've let me see that inner life and you can't drive me out again.'

It was true that she couldn't drive him out, but not in the way he thought.

'All right, you saw inside me,' she said at last. 'So keep my secrets.'

'Against anyone else,' he said at once. 'As long as you don't keep them against me.'

She shook her head, and her long fair hair fell about her face. He reached out to brush it back and was struck by something in her look. It was vulnerable and nervous, and it startled him into drawing a sharp breath.

She heard the sound, and misunderstood it as one of dismay.

Sapphire, she thought. Say what he might, that ghost was still with them. He'd brushed back the hair and seen the wrong face.

'You're fooling yourself,' she told him bitterly. 'She's not dead. She never will be.'

'I wasn't thinking of her—'

'You were doing more than thinking. You were looking for her—here.' She pointed to her face.

'Polly, I—where are you going?'

To his disbelief she leapt to her feet and rushed out of the little coffee bar, leaving him staring after her, too surprised to move.

'Get after her,' the man at the counter said. 'Pay me later.'

'Thanks, Tino,' he yelled, dashing out into the street and looking this way and that.

But she'd gone. In five seconds flat she'd managed to disappear.

Ruggiero ran, looking into the shops that were still open, but she wasn't there. He turned and ran to the other end of the street, but again he was unlucky.

It was impossible, but she'd completely vanished.

He began to walk, twisting this way and that, exploring side streets, all of them full of song and laughter that seemed to mock his confusion. Then he remembered her cellphone and drew out his own, ready to dial her number.

But he didn't know it. He nearly threw the phone away in disgust.

It was an hour before he walked despondently back to the coffee bar. She had probably returned home, and he would have to call and see if she was there, but there was just one last chance that she might have returned to the place where they'd started.

Even as he went in he knew it was a fruitless search. The bar was almost empty.

'Here's what I owe you,' he said, giving some money to Tino.

Then he realised that Tino was winking, and jerking his head at the corner. Ruggiero looked and saw a young woman with fair hair cropped close, a sleek, elegant head. She turned and gave him an appraising look.

'You—you—' He despised himself for stammering, but he couldn't help it.

She was an elfin creature—pretty, pert, with high cheekbones that he'd never noticed before and a neck that was almost swan-like. As he stood watching, struck to silence, she rose and sauntered past him to the door. One challenging glance over her shoulder, then she was gone.

A moment to get his breath and he was after her, catching her up in the street.

'Where were you?' he demanded, grasping her arm firmly. 'No, don't walk away.'

'Let go of me.'

'And risk you vanishing again? I don't think so. How did you manage to vanish into thin air?'

'I just went in there,' she said, indicating a barber shop right next to the coffee bar. 'It was the one place you never thought to look.'

'But that's a *male* barber's.'

'I know. They thought I was nuts, but I just said I wanted it off—all of it. Nothing fancy.'

'But—is it you?' he was peering at her.

'Yes, it's *me*,' she said, emphasising the last word.

'Do you mean,' he asked in mounting outrage, 'that I've been worried out of my mind about you and you've been having a haircut? Of all the crazy times to pick—'

'It was the perfect time. I should have done it long ago. You as good as told me that tonight.'

'*I*? I never said a word. Polly, have you been taking something? Because you're talking gibberish.'

'I'm talking about the way you looked at me tonight, trying to find Sapphire.'

He stared. 'Why have you got to drag her into this?'

'Because she's there. I saw it in your face.'

'If you did, you put her there yourself,' he said, becoming really angry. 'Why are you obsessed with her?'

'*I'm* not. You're the one who's haunted.'

'I told you—that's done with.'

'Yes, you keep telling me. Too often. Can you really dismiss a ghost that easily?'

'*I might if you'd let me.*'

She stared, thunderstruck.

'What?' she asked in a whisper.

'Don't you know that? It's a lot more complicated than you've realised.'

'Is it me?' she whispered. 'Is that really what's happening?'

'You bring her into every conversation.'

'Only because you—'

'No, don't push it onto *me*. I've fought my ghost, but yours is still there—and maybe she's harder to fight because she's been there all your life. All those comparisons you've told me about, with you always coming off worst. But why should you think like that? You were the brainy one, she needed you as much as you needed her. Who did who's homework?'

'But she was the one with the beauty and charm and—'

'Give me patience!' he groaned. 'Polly, did anyone ever tell you that you're an FCP?'

'What on earth is an FCP?'

'A Female Chauvinist Pig. You didn't know there was such a thing, did you? Hah! At least I've managed to take you by surprise. If a man implied that a woman should be defined by her looks rather than her brains he'd be condemned up hill and down dale, and probably sued as well. But you've just said exactly that. Polly, it's *nonsense*! You're a wonderful person—bright, funny and beautiful.'

'I'm not beau—'

'Don't say it,' he warned, wagging a finger in mock threat. 'Don't say you're not beautiful or I'll get annoyed.'

'Not in comparison to her—'

'But why must you always compare yourself to *her*?'

He read the answer in her expression and said, almost violently, 'She's not here. There's just you and me. I'm looking at *you*, and I tell you you're gorgeous. Why do you look at me like that?'

'Like what?'

'With that disbelieving expression, as though I was crying to the moon. Oh, to hell with everything!'

He'd grasped her shoulders before she knew what he meant to do, and his lips were on hers before she could protest. His arms were like steel rivets about her, and his lips were fierce and angry as they moved over hers again and again. It was a kiss without tenderness. The kiss of a man tearing down a brick wall to make his point. And it left her physically excited as nothing in her life had ever done before.

She tried to get sufficiently free to embrace him back, but before she could manage it he released her suddenly and stepped well away from her with a growl of fury.

'I'm sorry,' he said hoarsely. 'I'm sorry—I'm sorry. I—promised nothing like that would happen. I didn't mean to break my word, but—' He took a long, shaking breath. 'I guess the truth is I'm a bit of a bully.'

'A—a bully?' she asked, trying not to let her voice shake as much as his own.

'People have to see things my way, and if they don't I'll go to any lengths to make them. It's not nice and it makes me behave badly, but do you get the point now?'

'What—what point?' she stammered, wondering which universe she'd stumbled into.

'That you're beautiful. Did I convince you of that before I forgot my manners?'

For a wild moment she was temped to say no, and let him make the point again, and perhaps again. But common sense, the quality that always seemed to ruin things, intervened.

'I'm convinced,' she said, trying to laugh and failing. 'A practical demonstration is always useful.'

'You're angry with me.'

'No, I'm not.'

'You are. I can hear it in your voice—a terrible edge, as though you're wondering how much more of me you can stand. But don't worry. I'm on my best behaviour from now on.'

He neared her again, while still keeping a safe few inches between them, and she could sense that he was still trembling—almost as much as herself.

'I never really thought you looked like her,' he said, glancing at her shorn head. 'Not after that first mistake. But now—I don't know you at all.'

'Let's go from there.'

'Where to?'

'How about that meal you promised me? I'm starving.'

'It's not far away.'

In the next street they passed a jewellery shop, where something attracted him in the window. He drew her inside and made the proprietor show him the little brooch.

'A buttercup,' he said to Polly.

'Well, I told you they were everywhere. Common as muck.'

'Not this one. This is rare and valuable—perfect for you.'

Then Polly saw that the little flower was made of solid gold, and very expensive.

'I can't take this—' she gasped.

'You must. It might have been made for you.'

He pinned the brooch onto her dress and she realised that it did indeed look perfect, glowing under the lights as though it had were a glamorous flower instead of a prosaic one.

She twisted her head, trying to see her own shoulder, beaming with delight.

He led her to a tiny restaurant where the odours wafting out were delicious and the proprietor greeted him by name.

While they were eating *maccheroni* with Neapolitan ragù sauce Polly began to rub her neck self-consciously.

'What is it?' he asked.

'I must look very weird.'

'Not weird, but it's a little unsettling. And that's because you're a combination of someone I know and someone I've never met before. I'm definitely nervous.'

'So you should be,' she teased. 'I don't know the newcomer myself, so she might spring some surprises on both of us.'

'That'll be nothing compared with what it'll do to Brian.'

So absorbed was she in her new territory that she

almost said, Who? But she recollected herself in time.

'He's used to my funny ways,' she said vaguely.

'Oh, he's like that? Ready for anything? A man who can't be surprised, dominant, bestriding the world?'

'Stop it,' she said, laughing.

'You mean he's *not* like that? No, on second thoughts I picture him with glasses and the start of a paunch.'

'There's no need for you to picture him at all,' she said, trying to sound firm.

'But you never talk about him. For a man who's won your passionate love, he doesn't seem to make much impact on you.'

The memory of his kiss seemed to hang in the air between them. She was saved from having to answer by the waiter, bearing wine.

'Lacryma Christi del Vesuvio,' Ruggiero said as he poured it into her glass.

Suddenly she held out her hand across the table.

'Hallo,' she said, 'I'm Penelope. We've only just met.'

Ruggiero shook her hand.

'Indeed we have. So, Polly is short for Penelope?'

'Yes, they wanted to call me Penny when I was a kid. But I didn't like it so I became Polly.'

'I like Penelope,' he said, nodding. 'I learned about her in school: the wife of King Odysseus, who waited for him for twenty years. Penelope the faithful and wise.'

'Phooey—she was a twerp,' Polly said firmly. 'You wouldn't catch me waiting twenty years without even a postcard!'

He was unwise enough to answer this. 'They didn't have postcards in those—' He stopped as he caught her eyes on him, brimming with fun.

'But somehow I end up being wise despite trying not to be,' she said. 'At school it was always me warning the others that their daft pranks would lead to trouble, and then fibbing my head off to rescue them when it happened. I've always longed to be wild and outrageous. I try hard, I really do, but it doesn't come naturally to me. I planned all sorts of careers—actress, fashion designer, international bond saleswoman—anything, as long as I could rule the world.'

'But there are plenty of other people doing that,' he said, grinning as he refilled her glass. 'Be original.'

'Yeah, I make a great doormat.'

'Stop that,' he warned. 'You're talking like an FCP again, and I won't allow it.'

They clinked glasses, sharing their amusement, and for once Sapphire was nowhere.

'Anyway,' she said, glowing with joy at the warmth, the lights, the look in his eyes, and just possibly the wine, 'for tonight I'm just going to be Cinderella at the ball.'

'Is Cinderella ready for the next course?'

They passed on to to Neapolitan *rococo*—a sweet dish that seemed to contain everything from toasted almonds to candied peel of orange, flavoured with cinnamon, nutmeg, cloves. Polly closed her eyes in pure ecstasy.

'That's it,' Ruggiero said, satisfied. 'That's what I wanted to see. Have some more.'

'Yes, please!'

Their perfect accord continued until they were drinking coffee and liqueurs, when she happened to say, 'Talking as a nurse again, how are you managing now that you're back at work?'

'There's plenty to do. I'm not very popular at the moment, after wrecking our new prototype.'

'But that wasn't your fault.'

'It wasn't the machine's fault. It was working fine until I lost control. Everyone could see that, but they don't know why. The mechanics have been over everything again and again—but how do I tell them to stop bothering because it was only me seeing things that weren't there? I don't want them thinking I'm off my head, even if I am.'

'I can see that it might be a problem,' she admitted.

'And the next thing will be potential customers drawing back, wondering what's wrong with it.'

'What will you tell them?'

'Nothing. I'll have to demonstrate. It's lucky the rodeo is coming up.'

'Rodeo? With motorbikes?'

'Yes. We call it a rodeo, but actually it's a glorified bikers' meeting. It's a gathering of some of the best speedway riders in Italy, or even the world. We get riders from all over.'

'And they'll ride your machine to glory?' Polly asked.

He didn't answer, but she saw the wry look on his face and the truth hit her.

'Oh, no!' she said explosively. 'Definitely no. You can forget that idea right now.'

'It's what I have to do.'

'After what happened—'

'Especially after what happened. Just let them get the idea that one fall frightened me and the machine will get a bad name.'

'You mean *you'll* get a bad name,' she accused him. 'They'll say you're chicken.'

'Well, I certainly don't want to hear any clucking behind my back.'

'Let them cluck. You have more important things to consider. If you have one more fall like the last there's no knowing what will happen. How often do you think a man can land on his head without damaging his brains?'

A sulphurous silence.

'Why don't you add the next bit?' he demanded at last.

'What next bit?'

'The bit you're dying to say—*if he had any brains in the first place.*'

'I was being polite,' she said acidly.

'Why bother at this late date?'

It was astonishing how quickly a mood of sweet accord could descend into acrimony.

'Anyway, you've said it for me now,' she said crossly.

'Fine, I'm brainless—so there's nothing to damage. Polly, don't make so much of it. Nothing will happen. I'll be more careful this time.'

'Phooey! You're *never* careful.'

'You don't know that.'

'Anyone who's been acquainted with you for five minutes would know that. Ruggiero, listen to me—you are not going to do this, even if I have to stand in front of the bike to stop you.'

He regarded her sceptically. 'Cinderella didn't last very long, did she?'

'Cinderella never had to deal with a man who deluded himself with macho fantasies and had the common sense of a newt. And that's an insult to newts.'

He laughed at that, and Polly let the subject drop. But only because she planned to return to it at a more propitious time.

When it was time to leave Ruggiero didn't pay, but scribbled a note.

By now Polly was beginning to see a pattern.

'Let me guess,' she said as they left. 'You own half of this place as well. And probably several others.'

'Not half. Maybe a quarter here and there. It keeps me in touch with my friends. What is it?' He'd noticed her frowning.

'I just wondered if there's anything you own the *whole* of,' she mused.

'Not that I recall. Why? Does it matter?

'You've got a finger in so many pies, but you never risk your entire hand. Is that the answer? That you're reluctant to commit yourself totally? Always keeping something back?'

'Aren't you forgetting that I was willing to commit totally to Sapphire?'

'Were you? Are you so sure?'

'What do you mean by that?'

'I mean that it was never put to the test so you can believe what you like. Be honest, Ruggiero, we'll never know.'

He stopped and stared at her. 'Is that really what you think of me?'

'No, it's what I wonder about you. You blamed Sapphire because she didn't turn to you when she was ill. But maybe—' She checked herself and groaned. 'I did it, didn't I? I raised the ghost. You're right. I do it as often as you. Maybe more.'

Polly closed her eyes and pressed her hands to her forehead. 'Let me go,' she whispered to someone neither of them could see. *'Go away.'*

She turned, and would have started to run, but he grasped her quickly.

'No, I'm not going to lose sight of you again. You might never come back.'

'Perhaps it's better if I don't. My job here is nearly done. Let me go.'

'No,' he said drawing her close.

'Ruggiero,' she said, almost pleading. 'Don't—'

But the formal protest didn't fool him, as she had known it wouldn't. His lips were on hers, silencing her, saying all that needed to be said without words.

There was nothing to do now but banish regrets and yield herself up to the greatest joy she had ever known.

Everywhere the lights were going out, and when he drew her into a corner there was only darkness about them.

'Do you think I'm seeking her now?' he murmured. 'Can't you tell the difference?'

'I don't know.'

'Let her go, Polly. Until *you* drive her out neither of us can.'

He kissed her again and again, as though seeking the one kiss that would speak to her heart.

'Perhaps it can't be done,' she gasped.

'Don't say that,' he begged.

'I'm afraid. Aren't you?'

'*Yes.*'

She returned the kiss so that the impulse came from her and the strength was on her side. She was inexperienced in love, and the reverse was true of him, but now he was following her lead, learning from her, trusting her in love as in everything else.

But she was leading him along a road whose end was obscure to her—a road that might be wrong for both of them.

He guessed it too, for he said, 'You can deal with my ghost but can I deal with yours?'

'Hush.'

'Can Brian?' he growled. 'Does he even *know* that you still spend your life making comparisons? That when he kisses you he holds two women in his arms?'

'Forget him,' she urged.

'As you have?'

'He doesn't belong here now. Nobody else belongs here with us.'

She gave herself up to the joy of the moment, trying to believe that only this mattered and she could make it last for ever. But that hope was doomed. Even in the midst of her happiness she knew that.

It was the sound of a church bell that forced them back to reality, making them draw apart, both shaking with desire and confusion.

'Do you hear that?' she murmured.

'It's only the clock. Ignore it.'

'I can't. It's striking midnight. Time for Cinderella to go.'

'Why are you laughing?' he asked, feeling her shaking in his arms.

'I'm laughing at myself,' she said with a touch of hysteria. 'Oh, heavens! I should have remembered that midnight always comes. Sensible Polly isn't always so sensible after all.'

'I'm glad of that,' he said huskily.

He turned her face up and looked at it in the moonlight, seeing its clean, perfect lines as never before. The sight entranced him, and he would have kissed her again, but she pressed her hands against his chest.

'It's time we went home,' she whispered. 'The ball's over.'

'But you've left me a glass slipper, right?'

She shook her head. 'More like an army trainer. Nurse Bossy-Boots is back in charge.'

His smile was as sad as her own as they walked together back through the small, winding streets.

CHAPTER ELEVEN

'*DULL, dreary, prosaic. That's what I am, and I shouldn't have let myself forget it.*'

It was typical of the hand life had dealt Polly that after claiming her freedom by dramatically shearing off her hair she should find that it back-fired on her with a feverish cold.

'Can you take Matti?' she croaked to Hope next day. 'I don't want to get too close to him.'

The cot was promptly whisked out of her room, and she herself was banished back to bed, where she was nursed royally. Everyone looked in to wish her well—including Ruggiero, who stayed well back in response to her urgently flapping hands.

For three days she could do little but suffer. Her meals were brought upstairs, and in between eating she slept. At last she felt better, and began to make forays out of bed.

On one of these days she sat by the window, watching as Ruggiero, below, played with Matti, showing every sign of pride in his mental alertness, while his son, as always, strutted his stuff to an admiring audience.

They're both fine without me, she thought.

At that moment Hope pointed up to the window, and they all looked up, waving and smiling to her. For a strange moment it looked as if they were waving goodbye.

When she was sure she presented no threat to anyone, she went downstairs again.

'You were away too long,' Ruggiero told her.

'Or just long enough. You and Matti get on better when I'm not hovering over you.'

'I've taught him three new words. And Toni swears he's learning to call me Poppa, although it sounds more like *patata*.' He grinned. 'But I don't mind being called a potato by my son. He'll probably call me worse when he's older.'

'Brilliant. So now you and he have established a connection, you're not going to be taking any risks, are you?'

'Risks?'

'I can assume that you're enough of a father to abandon this mad idea of the rodeo?'

'It's tomorrow.'

'And you're riding?' she demanded, aghast.

'There's no reason why I shouldn't.'

'There's every reason. You're not fit yet. You'll

have another accident and maybe this time you'll be killed. That child has lost his mother—he doesn't deserve to lose his father too. Especially when he's only just met him.'

'It's no more than I've done before. I wasn't killed in the past, and what happened the day we met was a freak accident, and you know it. I have a duty to our workers to prove that the bike is good. They depend on us for a living.'

'So get another rider. You say there'll be others, so I expect any one of them would be glad of the chance.'

His mouth set in stubborn lines.

'It has to be me,' he said. 'Because I was the one riding when things went wrong.'

'And if things go wrong again—?'

Hope, approaching, overheard this and joined in the conversation with horror.

'I knew you were having this party, but I didn't know you were actually riding,' she said, appalled. 'You're not nearly well enough. Get one of the others to do it.'

'Don't give me orders, Mamma,' he said quietly. 'That goes for both of you.'

He walked away before either of them could reply.

Hope groaned and cursed herself.

'I'm sorry, *cara*. I shouldn't have spoken. You would have done much better.'

'But I wasn't doing any better,' Polly sighed. 'He's completely pig-headed. I don't understand that. I thought we were getting through to him— that *Matti* was getting through. Then suddenly everything goes into reverse. He plays with his son, he teaches him words, and he smiles in the right places, but he won't give up his pleasure to protect him. Oooh, I could—'

She made a strangling motion with her hands.

'Do it for both of us,' Hope snapped.

Secretly Polly knew that it was disappointment as much as anger that was driving her. The softened mood between herself and Ruggiero had seemed full of promise for his future with his son. Suddenly his image had darkened into that of a man concerned only with himself and his own wishes, without care for his child.

None of Ruggiero's siblings happened to be in Naples at that moment, so there was only Toni, Hope and Polly who might have attended the rodeo. Hope flatly refused to do so.

'No, you'll just be shopping nearby,' Ruggiero said. 'As always.'

'Not this time,' his mother declared. 'I'm going to stay here and look after your son. If you break your neck, you break your neck. That's your business.'

But when he'd left the house she turned to Polly

and said fearfully, 'You'll be there, won't you? If anything happens you'll look after him.'

'Of course. But he's probably right. Nothing will happen.'

She tried to sound reassuring, but she couldn't voice her real fear—that what had happened before would happen again and he would see something that wasn't there.

If it wasn't there.

'Leave him alone,' she whispered. 'You can't have him. Do you hear me?'

There was no answer. Either Sapphire had admitted defeat, or she was too sure of victory to bother arguing.

A privileged crowd had been allowed into the stands that surrounded the track. Potential buyers, a few journalists, every-one from the factory, plus friends and family from the biking fraternity.

In their company Ruggiero relaxed. He spoke the same language as these people—the language of speed and danger, the language of 'to hell with everything!' He'd been away from them too long, among people who didn't understand that risking your life was the most life-enhancing experience in the world. You had to toss it onto the flames to really enjoy the moment when you seized it back. What did they know?

There were ten riders, including Enrico, who had won more races than anyone else that season, and was eyeing the new bike hungrily.

'It's a bit soon for you to be riding again,' he said coaxingly. 'Take a longer rest.'

'I have to prove that bike. Not me, but the bike.'

It wasn't true. It was himself he had to prove again, but he couldn't admit that to anyone else.

The leather suit he'd worn before was now clean and perfect. When he put it on he felt he become himself again: his real self, the one he wanted to be, who'd almost been lost.

There was applause as five riders walked out for the first race. He knew they were all watching him, willing him to streak ahead on the new bike and leave the rest standing. Either that or get killed. One or the other. That was just how he liked it.

He stood for a moment, looking around through his visor, knowing the others were awaiting his move. From here he could just make out the place where she'd been before. It had been different then, with speed creating half the illusion, but now he needed no speed to conjure up the woman who stood before him.

Suddenly he became quite still, watching, understanding everything for the first time.

Then he began to move.

* * *

Toni drove Polly down to the track, left her there, and returned home on his wife's strict instructions. Polly was able to slip in and go to the same place in the stands where she had stood before.

The five bikes were already on the track, each with its own mechanic, waiting for the first race. Around her the crowd was abuzz with expectation. She couldn't understand the words, but she could guess their meaning.

She clenched her hands, waiting for things to start. But before anything could happen she heard the shrill of her cellphone. Pulling it out quickly, she found herself talking to Kyra Davis, a nurse she'd become friendly with two years earlier. Kyra was older, well on the road to promotion, and she had been there when Freda had died.

'I just called to say I've got my own ward at St Luke's,' she said, 'and I have two vacancies. I'd love you to fill one of them. Where are you now?'

'I'm in Italy.'

'But you'll come home soon, won't you? Pop over and we'll have a chat.'

'Can I call you back about that?' Her eyes were fixed on the track.

'Sure, just remember there's a job for you any time.'

She hung up.

There was a cheer. The bikers were coming out now. They all looked alike in their black leather and visors, but Polly would have known Ruggiero's tall, lean body anywhere.

Don't do it! Don't do it!

She saw him walk towards the bikes with the others, saw him stop and look around. His gaze seemed fixed on the place where she stood. He seemed transfixed, rooted to the spot, as though something was there that was revealed only to him.

What can you see?

Then a murmur went through the crowd as Ruggiero pulled off his helmet and turned to the man beside him, saying something. The murmur turned to a groan of disappointment as Ruggiero made a gesture indicating his bike. The other man let out a yell of delight and punched the air, but Ruggiero never saw it. He was already walking away.

He went on walking across the track until he came to the place where Polly stood, her eyes glistening, her heart overflowing.

'Enrico will ride for me,' he said. 'That's it. *Basta!*'

'What made you change your mind?' she asked, hardly able to get the words out. 'Did you see her?'

'No.' He shook his head. 'I saw you. And Matti was in your arms.'

* * *

'It's what you tried to tell me, isn't it?' he asked.

They were sitting in a small restaurant. After speaking to her Ruggiero had gone back to change out of his leather gear, giving her time to call Hope and tell her all was well.

Then they had left the track, finding the first place where they could sit together and talk quietly.

'I tried to find the words, but there aren't any,' Polly said.

'I had to learn it for myself,' he agreed. 'And now I have—just in that moment. I saw you holding Matti in your arms. The two of you were looking at me. But he wasn't really there, was he?'

'He's at home with your parents. But, yes—he *was* with me.'

He nodded slowly. 'And with me. For the first time I feel that he's mine.'

'And you are his,' she reminded him. 'Or it doesn't work.'

He took her hand. 'Let's go home.'

Hope and Toni were watching for them, standing on the steps with Matti between them, each holding one hand. They came down slowly, releasing him when they reached the ground, so that he had only to waddle two steps before clinging onto his father's leg for support.

Ruggiero dropped down to one knee to put his arms about his son.

'We got there,' he said huskily.

Polly stood back, watching them with pleasure, then exchanged glances with Hope and Toni. A decision was forming inside her.

She waited a few more hours, studying Ruggiero and Matti, but in her heart she was sure. These two had a road to travel yet, but they had found the start and placed their feet on it together.

She was even more certain when Ruggiero tried to assist his son in walking, holding his hand, and Matti impatiently thrust him away.

'There's a chip off the old block,' Toni said, and Ruggiero nodded.

'You used to fall over more often than not,' Hope reminded him.

'But he doesn't fall over,' Ruggiero said, regarding his child with pride.

At that moment Matti sat down hard.

'That was my fault,' Ruggiero hastened to say, speaking loud to be heard through his son's bawled indignation. 'He fell over my foot.'

At last Hope said, 'It's time this little one was in bed. Polly, shall we put him back in your room?'

'No, let him stay with you,' she replied quickly.

She joined the procession upstairs, but remained in the background during the ceremony as the last pieces of her resolution fell into place. Afterwards Ruggiero found her brooding on the terrace, and sat down, smiling contentedly.

She took a deep breath.

'I'm glad this has happened now,' she said. 'It makes it easy for me.'

'There's something in the way you say that that makes me nervous.'

'I have to go home for a while.'

'For a while? Are you coming back?'

She hesitated. 'I don't know. I need to be away from here, and you need to be alone with Matti. I'm starting to be in the way.'

'That's nonsense. I couldn't have got this far without you.'

'But you *have* reached this far, and you'll manage the next stage better if you let go of your nurse's hand.' She smiled. 'If you should need a hand to hold onto, take Matti's. You're both going in the same direction.'

'Matti needs you,' he insisted.

She waited, daring to hope. But Ruggiero didn't say that *he* needed her, and her heart sank again.

'I think Matti will be fine without me. This is his home now, and he loves it. He loves Hope and Toni and you.'

'He's getting used to me—'

'No, you're winning his heart. He's as bright as

a button, and he's just like his poppa. Everyone can see that. That's the bond. All you have to do is use it. You managed the big first step today.'

He didn't look at her as he said, in a strange voice, 'You're not doing this very well, Polly.'

'What do you mean?' she asked in alarm.

'You're doing what you once accused me of— just reciting the words. Why don't you tell me the real reason?'

For a moment she thought he'd guessed her feelings and was challenging her to speak them. And, if so, would it be so terrible to say that she loved him?

But then he added, 'I suppose Brian's cutting up rough, and you feel you have to get back to him?'

'Yes,' she said, letting out her breath slowly. 'It's Brian.'

'I wish I knew what you see in him. Isn't he worried about you?'

'I told you, he's a doctor.'

'Ah, yes—a man so busy serving humanity that he has no time for you. To hell with him! If he loved you, he'd be hammering on your door.'

'Not every man shows his feelings by tearing the walls down.'

'Just Neanderthals like me, huh?'

'I didn't—'

'Well, you're right. I told you how I went crazy in London when Sapphire vanished—roaming the streets, starving, half mad, knocking at doors. Why isn't *he* pounding doors for *you*?'

'Because for one thing he knows exactly where I am,' she replied in her most common sense voice.

'But does he know who you're with?'

'He knows I'm with a patient.'

'Does he know about this patient? How close we are? Does he know how I depend on you? That I've kissed you. Does he know that you've kissed me?'

'I didn't,' she said quickly. 'I didn't push you away because your ribs—'

'So that was a nurse's concern, was it? What about your other patients? Do you—?'

'Stop it,' she flashed, her eyes daring him to say any more. *'Stop right there.'*

He flushed.

'I'm sorry,' he muttered. 'I didn't mean to say that.'

'Never speak of this again. The sooner I go the better.'

She left quickly, before he could answer. Her breath was coming sharply, and every nerve in her seemed alive with conflicting emotions—anguish, temptation and desire contending with fear.

The fear was because she knew how close she'd come to yielding to what she must resist. Ruggiero wanted her to stay for Matti's sake, but also because his own nature needed her. It wasn't love, but for a woman who was passionately in love with him it might have been a bearable substitute.

Except for Sapphire.

He could say what he liked about being over her. It wasn't that simple. Her body might be dead, but still she would always be alive in the son they shared, in the memories that would live as long as his heart and soul lived.

And while that was true he could never really be hers.

What tormented her most was the knowledge that if she'd pushed matters, said the right words, she could probably have manoeuvred him into a proposal. But hell would freeze over before she did so. No half measures. He must be hers completely or not at all. Anything else would mean years of misery.

So the answer was not at all. And now she would flee this place, while she could still bear it.

Hope took the news of her impending departure calmly.

'Yes, you need to return for a while,' she said. 'Everything will still be here when you get back.'

'I'm not sure if I— I don't know how things will work out.'

Hope kissed her.

'We'll meet again,' she said placidly.

Her goodbye to Matti was tearful on her side but not on his. He'd perfected the art of putting shapes into the right holes and was eager to demonstrate.

'And he knows you'll be back soon,' Ruggiero said quietly.

'Perhaps. Are my things in the car?'

'Yes, I'm all ready to drive you to the airport, if you still want to go.'

I don't want to go, she told him silently. I want to stay with you always. I want to love you and have you love me. But you don't love me, and perhaps you never will. Maybe this is the only way I can find out.

'Yes,' she said, 'I still want to go.'

At the airport he carried her bags to Check-In, and walked with her towards the departure lounge.

'Stay,' he said suddenly. 'Don't go. You belong here.'

If he'd said, *Stay with me*, she would have done so, even then. But 'Stay' wasn't enough.

'I'm not sure where I belong,' she told him. 'I have to find out.'

'Will he meet you at the other end?'

'No, he's—'

'I know—he's busy,' Ruggiero interrupted her, exasperated. 'Then he has only himself to blame for anything that happens.'

He pulled her close and laid his lips on hers. Polly closed her eyes and gave herself up to the feeling for perhaps the last time. In this public place she couldn't embrace him as she wanted to, but she tried to let him know silently that her heart would remain here, although the rest of her might never return.

'Polly…' he said softly.

'I must go now. Goodbye.'

'We'll see each other again soon.' He was still holding her hand.

'Goodbye—goodbye—'

The little flat seemed to echo around her. The year spent there with her cousin and Matti had been terrible in many ways, but now that they were gone it was somehow worse. The emptiness struck her more fiercely for its contrast with the last few weeks in the cheerful villa, with members of the huge Rinucci clan wandering in and out.

She had nobody, she realised. Her only relative was Matti, and she'd parted with him for his own sake. She would visit him in Naples, and know herself to be welcome, but then she would come back here and the family doors would close behind her.

Why, that's it! she told herself. It's all of them I'm missing. Not only Ruggiero. I just loved being part of a big jolly family. I'm not in love with him. Not really.

With that settled it was easier to concentrate on settling in. She whisked around with a duster, bought herself some fish and chips from across the road, made a huge pot of tea and settled down to read the post that had arrived while she was away.

It was very silent. The scream of the phone was a relief.

'Did you have a safe journey?' Ruggiero asked from the other end.

'Yes, I'm fine, thank you.'

'Matti has been waiting for you to call and say you'd arrived. When you didn't, I told him I'd call you.'

Something caught in her throat, half-laughter, half tears.

'So the two of you had a nice little talk?' she asked.

'He did most of the talking. He wants to know how you are.'

'I'm just fine.'

'Was it a good flight? He knows you don't like flying, and he's worried about that.'

'Tell him it was a nice smooth flight.'

His voice became muffled as he turned away to say, 'She says it was a nice smooth flight.'

Matti answered, 'Aaaah!'

'He says he's very pleased,' Ruggiero passed on.

'Give him my love.'

'Why don't you tell him yourself? Here, Matti. Put it to your ear—like that.'

'Aaaah!' he said.

'Is that you, darling?' she asked.

'*Si, si, si, si, si.*'

'You've learned another word. How clever you are.'

'Aaaah!'

'He says he loves you,' came Ruggiero's voice. 'He wants you to say it too. Here, Matti.'

'I love you,' she said softly. 'Matti?'

'He slid off my lap and went to Mamma,' Ruggiero said.

'It's time he was in bed.'

'She's just about to take him.'

'And you?'

'I'll be there, too.'

'Good. I must go now. Goodnight.'

'*Ciao!*'

'*Ciao!*'

She put down the phone and sat quietly in the dusk, until there was no light left.

CHAPTER TWELVE

THERE'S a letter for you,' Hope said, putting it in Ruggiero's hand. 'From England.'

Conscious of his parent's eyes fixed eagerly on him, he pulled open the envelope. Inside was a letter and a photograph, showing a small headstone in a graveyard. Beneath it was the name of the church and the village.

I found this when I got home. One day Matti might like to have it. Talk to him about her. Remember what I told you—that she was a good mother and she loved him with all her heart, until the last moment of her life. Think of her like that, and try to forgive her the rest.

It was signed, *'Your affectionate Bossy-Boots.'*

'She talks as though she wasn't coming back,' Hope observed.

'I don't think she is,' Ruggiero said heavily.

'And you're just going to accept that?' Hope demanded, outraged. 'Why didn't you ask her to marry you?'

'Have you forgotten that she's engaged?'

'Poof! Don't tell me you're going to let yourself be put off by a trifle like that?'

'Mamma,' he said with a faint grin, 'sometimes I think you're completely immoral.'

'I can remember when, if you wanted a woman, you'd have elbowed a whole army of fiancés out of your way.'

'Well, perhaps it's time I stopped doing such things. Other people have rights.' He gave a grunt. 'I guess I finally learned that.'

'Not from me. I tried but I failed there.'

'No—from her. It's odd,' he said softly, 'but when I think of all the things I learned from her it really makes her seem like Nurse Bossy-Boots. And yet...' He paused and smiled faintly, as though he barely realised he was doing so. 'She wasn't a bit like that.'

'What was she like?' Hope asked, her gaze fixed fondly on him.

He shook his head. 'I can't tell. Even to me she's—I don't know.'

'But what does she say on the phone? You call her every night.'

'Matti calls her every night,' he corrected fondly.

'They talk and I put in the odd word. I'm not sure she'd talk to me as easily. Now she's with her fiancé again...' Ruggiero sighed. 'Heaven knows what kind of man he is, but she seems very set on him.'

'She told you that?'

'No, she gave me only bare details. If I ventured onto that territory I got ordered off.'

'Hmm!'

'Mamma, you can put more meaning into that one little sound than anyone I know.'

'Has it ever occurred to you that this man may not exist? That he may be simply a device she has found useful?'

He nodded. 'At the start I wanted her to keep Matti, but I had to give up when she mentioned the fiancé, and it did cross my mind that she'd invented him to silence me. But when she returned from England with you he called her.'

'She said so?' Hope demanded sceptically.

'No, but I heard her say something about a hospital. And since he works in one—'

'That could have meant anything. Her friends had to return Matti early because their daughter had been rushed to hospital. Perhaps she was talking to them?'

'But you told me she went out to see him while you were there.'

'I said she went out for a couple of hours. I don't know who she saw.'

'But he was there when I called her the other night.'

Hope turned, thoroughly startled now. 'She actually told you that?'

'No, but I heard him in the background, asking where she kept the glasses.'

She breathed again.

'And it didn't occur to you that if he were her fiancé he'd have known that without asking?'

'You think—? No, there could be many things to account for it.'

'You won't know unless you go to find out.'

Unwittingly, she'd touched a nerve. Suddenly he was back in London, searching uselessly for someone who wasn't there, turning corner after corner, always hoping that he would find his dream around the next one. An icy dread went through him at the thought of doing it again.

He didn't call her that night, hoping she would call him. But the phone was silent. And when the next night came he found that he couldn't force himself to call. The silence of the evening before held him in a grip of dread. The next night he admitted to himself that he was afraid, and the admission was a kind of release, so that he snatched up the receiver and dialled her home number.

The phone was dead.

There was still her cellphone, but that had been switched off. He called it repeatedly over the next twenty-four hours, but it was always off.

She had vanished into thin air.

Hope had given Ruggiero the address. All he had to do was take a taxi from London Airport to the building where her tiny apartment was situated. He arrived in the late afternoon. As he got out he looked up at the window on the second floor, which Hope had said was hers. He couldn't be sure, but he thought he saw the curtain twitch.

Seeing someone come out of the front door, he took the chance to slip inside, and began to climb the stairs. There was only one door on the second floor and he knocked at it.

It was opened by the most handsome young man Ruggiero had ever seen.

He was in his late twenties, with tousled hair and a cheerful face. He was also wearing a towelling robe, as if he'd just got out of the bath.

'Hi, can I help you?' he asked.

Ruggiero felt himself engulfed by hell. It was the voice he'd overheard on the telephone, and this young man was built like a god.

'No, thank you,' he said hurriedly. 'I think I've come to the wrong place.'

'Maybe not. I've only just moved in, so perhaps you're thinking of— Coming, darling.'

He called this over his shoulder. Ruggiero knew he had to get away fast.

'Who is it, darling?' A female voice floated from within.

But it wasn't *her* voice. Suddenly his legs were paralysed with relief.

A young woman, also in a bathrobe, appeared. She was nothing like Polly.

'I'm looking for Polly Hanson,' he managed to say.

'Oh, you mean the woman who lived here before?' the girl said. 'She moved out a few days ago.'

'It was very sudden,' the young man said. 'She wanted to move, and we needed somewhere quickly, so we dropped in one evening to look the place over.'

'You mean—you're not Brian?'

'Brian? No, my name's Peter. I don't think I've heard of Brian. Polly didn't mention a Brian, did she, Nora?'

'Not that I heard.'

The hell that had engulfed Ruggiero retreated very slightly.

'Did she leave a forwarding address?'

'She only mentioned a hotel,' Nora said. 'The Hunting Horn, I think it was. Not far away.'

A taxi took him to the hotel. He sat in the back, telling himself not to be fanciful. Just because she'd vanished and he was looking for her at a hotel, like last time, that didn't mean—

She was no longer at the Hunting Horn.

'She stayed just three days,' the pretty receptionist explained. 'No, I'm afraid she didn't say where she'd be after that.'

Now his forehead was damp, and desperation was growing inside him. History was repeating itself, drowning him again.

'Try St Luke's Hospital,' the receptionist. 'She said she worked there once, and she might be going back.'

'Thank you,' he said frantically.

Another taxi. Another desperate journey. Trying to tell himself that this time it would be different. There was the hospital, a huge building, just up ahead. He leapt out and almost ran inside.

For a moment he thought he was in luck. The man on the desk remembered Polly.

'She was here a few days ago. You might try—' He named a ward and directed him to it.

As he approached the ward a nurse in her mid-thirties emerged and halted him.

'I'm afraid visiting isn't until this evening,' she said, in a voice that was pleasant but firm.

'Please, I'm not visiting. I'm looking for Polly Hanson.'

'She's not here.'

Darkness again, blanking out everything except the road ahead that wound around endless corners, leading to nothing.

'I was told she worked here,' he said, his mouth dry.

'I hope she soon will be. I called her in Italy and tried to persuade her to come back here—because we really need nurses like her—but she said she had something urgent to do before she finally made up her mind.'

'You know her, then?'

'I'm an old friend. My name's Kyra Davis, and I got to know her very well the last time she was here.'

'She worked in this part of the hospital?'

'Yes, but I meant when her cousin was dying. Oh, dear—maybe I shouldn't be telling you all this. I don't know who you are.'

'I'm the father of her cousin's child.'

'You mean Matthew? She used to bring him in to see his mother in the last days. We managed to find a little side ward for her, so that they could all be together in peace.'

'It's here?' he asked, looking around.

'Yes, It's empty just now, so you can see it if you like.'

As she opened the door to the side ward her beeper went.

'I think someone wants me,' she said, and bustled away, leaving him alone in the room.

It was small, plain and bare, except for the sunshine streaming onto the empty bed. Ruggiero stared at it, trying to understand that this was the place where Sapphire had died.

Only a few weeks ago she had lain in that bed, looking at this room. He tried to picture her, but there was nothing.

Nothing!

But Polly was present, sitting on the chair, pushed up close to the bed so that she could place Matti in his mother's arms while still holding him for safety. She'd sat there hour after hour, her arms around both of them, growing tired, her body aching, her heart grieving, enduring it all so that mother and child could have those last precious moments together.

How did he know that? She'd never told him. But he knew it was true because he knew her. In those last hours and moments every fibre of her being had been concentrated on helping the people in her care, with never a thought for herself.

'Polly—are you still there? I can't see you.'

'Yes, darling. I'm always here. Feel my hand.'

'You won't forget—you'll find him—and tell him about the baby—'

'*I'll find him—I'll make sure they know each other—*'

'*Where are you? Don't let me go.*'

'*I'm here—hold onto me—feel my arms around you—hold on—*'

Dazed, he looked around. How could he hear them when they weren't there?

Not true.

Sapphire had never existed.

But Polly was there. She would be there in his heart for ever, her arms outstretched in generous giving, the only way she knew to live.

The winding road had finally reached its destination—this little room, where one journey had ended and another had begun, like a torch being passed from hand to hand.

'Are you all right?' the nurse asked from the doorway.

'Yes, I'm fine,' he said joyfully. 'I've never been better. But I have to talk to her.'

'She said she was going away for a few days.'

'With Brian?' he asked, scarcely breathing.

'Who?'

'Her fiancé.'

'Polly doesn't have a fiancé. She's in love with a man who doesn't feel the same way. That's all she'd tell me.' She eyed Ruggiero curiously, but was too tactful to say more. She only added, 'I think she's gone to Yorkshire—back to her old village.'

'Thank you. I can find her now.'

At the station he caught a train north. From there it was a bus ride to the little village, and by good fortune the bus stopped close to the church.

It was dark, but it was a tiny place, and, using the picture Polly had given him, he managed to locate the right corner of the graveyard. There was the little slab, with Freda's name and the dates of her life. He glanced at them only briefly. He was looking for something else.

But he was alone. There was no sign of Polly. Only some flowers on the grave suggested that she'd been there.

He was back on the endless road, seeking something that was always out of sight around the next corner, until there were no more corners left.

'No,' he muttered. 'Not this time.'

He looked around the graveyard, searching in the poor light until he finally found what he was looking for. By now he was at the edge of the ground, with a clear view across the road, where a flower shop was just closing. Ruggiero sprinted across, just managed to get his hand in the door, and engaged in the most desperately important negotiation of his life.

* * *

It had taken a couple of days for Polly go around the old places—the home where she'd lived as a child, the second home when her aunt and uncle had taken her in, the school where she'd done so well, passing her exams with flying colours and helping Freda, whose skills had lain in another direction.

She would have liked to avoid Ranley Manor, but her route had happened to lie that way, so she'd hurried past. Even so she had been unlucky enough to see George handing a young woman into his chauffeured car.

She'd gone to see Freda within an hour of her arrival. She'd wanted to tell her cousin that she'd kept her promise. When she'd laid the violets on the grave she'd said, 'I'll be back tomorrow.'

Next day she'd brought lilies to replace the violets. She had stayed for a while, talking about Matti.

'He'll be all right, I promise,' she'd said. 'You were right to send him to Ruggiero. He's going to be a great father. I'm going tomorrow, but I'll be back here before I go—just once more.'

She was keeping her promise, bearing more flowers, but as she ran the last few steps to lay them down she stopped suddenly and stared.

The grave was covered in buttercups, glorious

brilliant yellow and gold buttercups, flaunting their rich, extravagant beauty to the world.

Looking around her, she saw that not a buttercup was left growing in the grass. Someone had determinedly plucked every last one to lay them here in a silent message.

Then she saw that the yellow flowers were not alone. A corner of the grave was given up to tea roses.

And she was back again in the little restaurant in Naples, talking about flowers and their meaning.

Tea roses—in peaceful memory. All passion spent. All forgiven and only the best remembered.

But it was the buttercups that lay in joyous profusion, carrying their message of love, acceptance, freedom to go on living and loving.

Ruggiero appeared so suddenly that she guessed he'd been waiting for her. He was unshaven and his suit was creased, as though he'd been sleeping on the ground, and his eyes were full of a troubled question.

But before he could ask the question she answered it, opening her arms so that he ran to her at once, his own arms flung wide to seize her and draw her close.

'Why did you leave me?' he asked hoarsely. *'Where have you been?'*

'I had to go,' she cried, holding onto him. 'I had to find out if what I was afraid of was true.'

He silenced her mouth with his own, and it was a long time before he could breathe enough to say, 'You should have trusted me.'

'It's not that—I didn't know how you really felt. I thought you might let me go and realise that it was for the best.'

'How could it be best for me to lose you?' he demanded passionately. But then a change came over him. He grew calmer and shook his head. 'But you didn't really think I'd let you go,' he said. 'You couldn't have. In your heart you know everything there is between us. Don't you?'

He was right, she realised. Some part of her had known that he would come after her because he loved her. Hearing it said now, she recognised the truth. He knew her better than she knew herself.

'Everything,' he repeated. 'Now and always. It took us both a little time to see it, but it was always there.'

He drew her close again, not in a kiss, but in a whole-hearted embrace, arms tight about each other, totally committed, nothing held back. For a long time neither of them moved or spoke

There was a small commotion as a crowd of schoolchildren appeared and headed in their direction.

'Come away,' he said, drawing her towards the ancient little church.

They found privacy in the old wooden porch, where they could sit apart from the world, yet still able to see the flowers with their glowing promise of hope.

'You look terrible,' she said, touching his unshaven chin

'I spent the night here. I couldn't risk missing you. I only left for a few minutes, to get the roses I'd ordered from a shop across the road, but I got back fast. I've been waiting here, watching. I was so afraid you wouldn't come back at all.'

'I had to say a proper goodbye to her before I finally decided where I was going next.'

'Back to Brian?' he asked belligerently.

'There's no Brian, and you know that perfectly well.'

'I just wanted to hear you say it,' he growled, holding her tight, almost as if he was afraid 'Brian' would appear and snatch her away.

'He was just a device to make you concentrate on Matti,' she admitted. 'But then I found him useful, helping me to keep everything impersonal. I didn't want you to think of me as a woman. Or,' she added, seeing his raised eyebrows and hint of a smile, 'maybe I wanted it too much. One of the two. I couldn't decide which. I thought he'd fade into the background, but you kept on about him.'

'I was jealous as hell. I could have throttled him because you loved him. All the time I could feel us getting closer, and I didn't know what to believe. When you left I thought you'd gone back to him.'

'I didn't just want to be a substitute for Freda, and I was afraid I'd never know if I was or not. I couldn't live with second best. It has to be all or nothing.'

He nodded.

'I thought we'd both have time to think, but when I reached England—' she gave a shaky laugh '—a terrible thing happened. I had an attack of common sense.'

'You should have known better. What has common sense to do with us?'

'Everything seemed so clear. You had Matti, and you didn't need me any more. I wanted to break completely with the past, so I gave up my flat and got out so that the new people could move in quickly. I've got a job offer at the hospital.'

'I know. I was there.'

'You went to the hospital?'

'I saw the room where she died. I stood there and looked around, and all I could see was you. Wherever I am I see only you, and that's how it will be—all my life. But I didn't understand at first. The way we met—she was always between us. I lived in confusion for so long. If you hadn't come I don't know what would have happened to me. I was caught up in a kind of madness, and you released me. Now I'm free—truly free at last. It feels like starting life again.

'Sapphire—'

'Freda,' he said at once. 'There was no Sapphire.' He saw her looking at him, and said, 'But now I can be grateful to her. I can even love her memory for Matti's sake.'

'I'm glad of that,' she said fervently. 'Because one day you'll bring him here—'

'We'll bring him together, and tell him about her.'

They were silent, thinking of that moment.

'We might even bring our own children as well,' he mused.

'You've got it planned?'

'Matti has. He wants brothers and sisters. He's a Rinucci; he likes being part of a big family.'

She smiled tenderly and leaned her head against him.

'He told you that, did he?' she asked.

'Sure he did. We understand each other perfectly these days. He also says that if I don't bring you back with me I needn't bother coming home.

He was very plain about that—threw his cereal bowl against the wall.'

They laughed together for a moment, but then he took her hand and carried it to his lips.

'Promise that this hand will always be in mine,' he whispered.

'Keeping you safe?'

'No, leading me to the best of life. Even when you stopped me riding the bike you weren't restraining me, just showing me a different way forward. We'll go wherever the road winds, and as long as it's you that takes me there I know it'll be a good place.'

They walked back to the grave and stood for a moment, looking at the flowers—tea roses and buttercups—side by side in perfect harmony.

'You understand, don't you?' he asked softly. 'Please say that you do?'

She nodded. 'Thank you. Not just for my flowers, but for hers.'

'They had to come first. I know that now.' He smiled suddenly. 'You're wearing yours,' he said, indicating the gold brooch on her shoulder.

'I always wear it.'

'Promise me that you always will?'

'I promise—for ever.'

She leaned down and took two of the flowers,

one of each, putting them away to be kept, also for ever. All done now. All answered. All forgiven.

He kissed her gently, knowing that everything else must wait a little. But they could afford to wait.

Nor did they look back as they walked away. There was no need. They knew the flowers were blooming brightly in the morning sun.

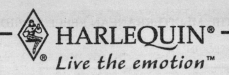

HARLEQUIN®
Live the emotion™

 American ROMANCE®

Heart, Home & Happiness

⟨⟩ HARLEQUIN® *Blaze*™

Red-hot reads.

⟨⟩ HARLEQUIN®

EVERLASTING LOVE™

Every great love has a story to tell™

 **Hi** Harlequin® Historical
Historical Romantic Adventure!

⟨⟩ HARLEQUIN®

HARLEQUIN ROMANCE®

From the Heart, For the Heart

⟨⟩ HARLEQUIN®

INTRIGUE

Breathtaking Romantic Suspense

Medical Romance™...
love is just a heartbeat away

 N**e**xt™

**There's the life you planned.
And there's what comes next.**

⟨⟩ HARLEQUIN®
Presents
Seduction and Passion Guaranteed!

⟨⟩ HARLEQUIN®
SuperRomance®

Exciting, Emotional, Unexpected

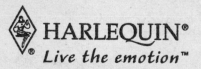

HARLEQUIN®
INTRIGUE®

BREATHTAKING ROMANTIC SUSPENSE

Shared dangers and passions lead to electrifying romance and heart-stopping suspense!

Every month, you'll meet six new heroes who are guaranteed to make your spine tingle and your pulse pound. With them you'll enter into the exciting world of Harlequin Intrigue— where your life is on the line and so is your heart!

THAT'S INTRIGUE— ROMANTIC SUSPENSE AT ITS BEST!

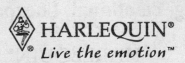

HARLEQUIN®
Live the emotion™

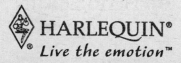

HARLEQUIN®
Presents®

The world's bestselling romance series...
The series that brings you your favorite authors,
month after month:

Helen Bianchin...Emma Darcy
Lynne Graham...Penny Jordan
Miranda Lee...Sandra Marton
Anne Mather...Carole Mortimer
Susan Napier...Michelle Reid

and many more uniquely talented authors!

Wealthy, powerful, gorgeous men...
Women who have feelings just like your own...
The stories you love, set in exotic, glamorous locations...

HARLEQUIN®
Presents®

Seduction and Passion Guaranteed!

HPDIR104

Harlequin® Historical
Historical Romantic Adventure!

Imagine a time of chivalrous knights and unconventional ladies, roguish rakes and impetuous heiresses, rugged cowboys and spirited frontierswomen—these rich and vivid tales will capture your imagination!

Harlequin Historical... they're too good to miss!